What in the

Isaiah braced his hands ag[...]
and lowered his head until it touched Sandra's front door.

He'd spent hours trying to talk himself out of coming here, staying at the rec center long after the party had ended.

It hadn't worked.

"Go home," he whispered. She'd never have to know he had come here.

But his body refused the direct order. It stood steadfast at the door, not caring about the fact that he had no reasonable explanation for being there or the very real possibility of Sandra slamming the door in his face.

All Isaiah knew was he had to see her again.

Now.

Exhaling, he slid one hand down to the doorbell and pressed. The chime preceded one of the longest minutes of his life.

"Forget something?" he heard her ask through the door before it swung open.

Sandra held out the blue diaper bag he'd seen slung over her shoulder earlier. He watched her brown eyes widen at the sight of him.

Before either of them had time to think, Isaiah wrapped an arm around her waist and pulled her to him. She gasped as she stared up at him, and he caught the scent of cotton candy on her breath.

"Yeah, I forgot this."

He leaned in and captured those pouty lips of hers—lips that had played a starring role in his dreams for four nights straight—in a kiss.

Books by Phyllis Bourne

Harlequin Kimani Romance

Taste for Temptation
Sweeter Temptation
Every Road to You
Falling into Forever

PHYLLIS BOURNE

is a native of Chicago's South Side and began her writing career as a newspaper crime reporter. After years of cops and criminals, she left reporting to write about life's sweeter side. Nowadays, her stories are filled with heart-stopping heroes and happy endings. When she's not writing, she can usually be found at a makeup counter feeding her lipstick addiction.

You can find her on the web at www.phyllisbourne.com and www.facebook.com/phyllisbournebooks.

Falling into Forever

PHYLLIS BOURNE

HARLEQUIN® KIMANI™ ROMANCE

For Byron, who shoulders the heavy lifting
so I can live my dream.

Recycling programs
for this product may
not exist in your area.

ISBN-13: 978-0-373-86378-5

Falling into Forever

Copyright © 2014 by Harlequin Books S.A.

Printed in U.S.A.

Dear Reader,

Family is the best thing about the Thanksgiving holiday—
it can also be the worst.

In *Falling into Forever* Sandra's and Isaiah's parents are
overbearing, embarrassing and hilariously obnoxious.
They're also loyal, loving and filled with high expectations
for their offspring.

While *Falling into Forever* is foremost a romance,
at heart it's a story about us as children—from toddlers
to gray-haired adults with kids and grandkids of our own.
We never lose our desire to make our parents proud.

Have a wonderful Thanksgiving!

Phyllis

I'd like to thank my fellow authors in the
Wintersage Weddings continuity series, A.C. Arthur and
Farrah Rochon, for their support and encouragement.
You ladies are the best!

Chapter 1

"I want that low-down, cheating bastard to eat his heart out."

The edict echoing in her head, Sandra Woolcott swept the graphite pencil over the paper in bold, rapid strokes. Turning a client's dream dress into reality was her business.

Still, this particular request was a first.

A revenge dress.

Sandra sat cross-legged on her living room sofa, sketch pad on her lap, and examined the illustration. A sleek, backless dress with a thigh-exposing split. Sexy and beautiful, the gown encapsulated the hallmarks of a garment worthy of bearing her Swoon Couture label.

She stuck the pencil behind her ear and gnawed at her bottom lip as she continued to study the sketch. Her client had a lot riding on this particular dress.

It had to be better than good. It had to be perfect.

She ripped the page from the sketch pad, crumpled it into a ball and tossed it in the direction of a wastebasket stationed near the sofa. It landed on the hardwood floor in a pile of similar wads filled with rejected ideas.

Sandra scrubbed a hand down her face in frustration.

She worked by appointment only, with a private clientele, her schedule packed months ahead with back-to-back appointments for consultations and fittings. She also had to handle the business end of running her custom shop.

Mondays were the day of the workweek Sandra focused solely on the creative side of Swoon Couture.

Instead of retreating to the studio at her shop, she'd decided to work from home, hoping a change of scenery would help her get caught up on the tasks she'd put on hold last week to help arrange her friend Janelle's wedding.

No such luck.

She'd barely made a dent in her to-do list, which included ideas for Everley Madison, a pop singer she was scheduled to meet with in a few days to discuss a gown for her New Year's Eve wedding, and the preliminary designs for clients preparing for the spring season of charity balls.

Instead, she'd spent the majority of the day stumped on the last-minute plea from one of the most prominent citizens of Wintersage, Massachusetts.

"We built that business together. Now he expects me to sit home alone while he strolls into the party celebrating its silver anniversary with his new skank on his arm," Octavia Hall had complained during her design consultation. "A party I spent over a year planning. I didn't even use Alluring Affairs, because I wanted to see to every detail personally."

Sandra had listened patiently while Octavia spent the entire hour painstakingly listing her soon-to-be ex's faults, without giving as much as a clue to the style of dress she wanted.

It didn't matter.

Behind the older woman's bravado, longing had lurked in her eyes. It told Sandra that, deep down, her client was really seeking a gown so breathtaking, the sight of her in it would make her estranged husband think twice about abandoning their marriage for a twenty-year-old.

It was a lofty goal for a dress. However, Sandra intended to do everything within her power to make Octavia, a former Miss Massachusetts, once again the most stunning woman in the room.

The clock on the mantel over the fireplace chimed, and Sandra calculated she could squeeze in another hour of work before making the short walk from her house, overlooking the harbor, to The Quarterdeck for her weekly business meeting/gossip session with her two best friends and business partners. In the meantime, she needed to concentrate on coming up with a showstopper of a gown.

She stared at the blank sketch-pad page. A vague idea of a shimmering dress embellished with beads and sequins…no, satin in the same caramel tones as Octavia's skin…danced on the edge of Sandra's imagination.

She closed her eyes and focused as the details slowly unfolded. Excited, she opened her eyes and snatched the pencil from behind her ear. She needed to get this design down on paper quickly, while it was fresh in her mind.

The doorbell sounded. Both the jarring chime and the accompanying pounding on her front door jerked Sandra from her thoughts, and visions of the satin gown faded.

So much for thinking working from home was a good idea. Muttering a curse, she set the pencil and pad aside.

She peered through the peephole and frowned. What were her parents doing in town?

"I thought you two were in New York City." Sandra shivered against a blast of late-October wind coming off the nearby Atlantic Ocean as she pushed the door closed behind them.

"We barely had time to visit with the Kings before your father began griping about getting back to Wintersage and returning to work," Nancy Woolcott said, "and his *girlfriend*."

Stuart Woolcott winked at his wife. "Don't be jealous of my side piece. She may be sexy, but you're still my number one."

As they walked into her living room, Sandra couldn't help smiling at her parents' running joke over her dad's prized 1970 Chevy Chevelle SS. He'd acquired the muscle car of his boyhood dreams back when Sandra was in elementary school, and the rare hours he wasn't in his office he spent in the garage, restoring his *girlfriend* to her seventies glory.

"I got a call about a 454 engine. I need to take a look at it," he said. "Afterward, I'm going into the office."

"That office isn't going anywhere. Surely it can wait until tomorrow morning," her mother countered.

"Woolcott Industries doesn't run itself, dear. And neither of our children can be bothered to help run it, either."

Sandra felt her father's pointed stare as she bussed her mother's upturned cheek.

Here we go, she thought, and steeled herself for the lengthy lecture that always accompanied that look. Sure enough, he launched into it.

"Computer hardware was good enough for me, my father, my grandfather and his father, who started out selling typewriters and adding machines, but it's not good enough for my kids." Her dad walked past her into the living room. "Fred King's daughter, Ivy, is vice president of his company, you know. Her husband also works for their company, and they've given Fred two beautiful grand—"

"Don't start, Stu." Her mother cut him off. "Sandra chose her career. When the time comes, she'll choose a husband and when to have children."

"She's not getting any younger," Stuart said, as if twenty-eight years old was ancient. "And I just happen to know Dale Mills has asked our daughter out several times."

Sandra cringed inwardly at the mention of the Woolcott Industries' executive. Every sentence the man uttered was bracketed with the words, *Stuart says* or *Stuart advises.*

No way she'd ever date that brownnosing suck-up.

"Dale's a good-looking young man," her mother added. "And so considerate. Last week, he stood in line overnight just so he could surprise your father with Red Sox tickets for game two of the World Series."

Sandra willed her eyes not to roll. She looked away

from her mother to see her father scooping a wadded sheet from her sketch pad off the floor.

Unfurling it, he frowned. "Just think, Fred's daughter's negotiating multimillion-dollar deals."

Sandra reached out to snatch the discarded sketch from his grasp.

Her father shook his head. "Meanwhile, my daughter is determined to make her living doodling stick figures."

Sandra stopped short as a long forgotten voice and a buried memory pushed their way to the surface.

"*Whatcha doing, doodling stick figures?*" a boy looking over her shoulder in her high school art class had asked.

Sandra remembered spinning around, prepared to give him a piece of her mind. Instead, her angry gaze had locked with the dreamy brown eyes of Isaiah Jacobs, one of the most popular boys at Wintersage Academy.

One smile from him had turned her insides to mush, and all Sandra could do was gawk openmouthed. When she'd finally spoken, her tongue had twisted and her words had spilled out in a jumble.

Sandra sighed. Isaiah had gone on to become her first boyfriend, her first love and her first heartbreak.

"Stu!" Her mother's sharp tone roused Sandra from the errant flashback.

"What?" Her father raised his hands in the air, his expression perplexed. "The girl tested off the charts in math and science, but instead of being an asset to her family's business, like Ivy, she squanders her natural ability as a *dressmaker.*" He made the word *dressmaker* sound like *loser.* "How am I the bad guy here?"

Frowning at her husband, Nancy snatched the sketch

from his hand and placed it on an end table. "You start this up every time we visit the Kings," she said. "Let. It. Go."

Sandra shot her mom a grateful look. The fact that Swoon Couture specialized in custom dresses and catered to the wealthiest women in Wintersage was lost on her father. As far as Stuart Woolcott was concerned, if Sandra didn't work for Woolcott Industries, she didn't really work.

Noticing the garment bag draped over her mother's arm, Sandra jumped at the chance to change the subject. "I see you had time to do some shopping."

Nancy averted her eyes. "Uh…well, I found a few things, including the most adorable Halloween costume for little Mason. He's going to be a Patriots' player."

While her mother prattled on about toddler football helmets, Sandra zeroed in on the garment bag. In particular, the embossed logo of a hot New York designer who'd been getting incredible buzz in the fashion world. It was obvious the contents weren't for Sandra's nephew.

"I know this is a busy time of year for you with the holiday season almost upon us. I thought I'd take some of the pressure off by trying a new designer I read about in *Vogue* magazine," her mother said, in way of explanation. "In fact, he's been in all the magazines."

"B-but I already have a capsule collection of holiday dresses, designed especially for you." As always, Sandra had prioritized her mother's dresses, having nailed down the perfect cuts, colors and styles for her over the summer. "They're waiting for you at the boutique."

"I'm sure they're beautiful as always, dear, but everybody who's anybody in Wintersage will be wearing *your* gowns this holiday season. No one will have Zack originals."

"So you brought the dresses to show me?" Sandra asked, trying hard to keep the slighted edge out of her voice.

To be honest, she was also curious to see what the competition offered that was so dazzling her mother had purchased off-the-rack dresses without even bothering to see the custom ones Sandra had prepared.

"Not exactly." Nancy glanced uncomfortably at the garment bag. "Actually, I was hoping to drop them off with you."

"I don't understand. Why would you need to bring them to me?" Sandra asked, confused.

"W-well, you see, your father was in such a hurry to get back home, I didn't have time for a fitting and alterations," her mother stammered. "I thought, well, since you know my measurements. I only need two inches off the bottom of all of them and a little nip at the waist of the green one…"

Nancy held the garment bag out to her, and Sandra's jaw dropped as realization dawned. Her mom expected her to handle the alterations.

Stuart took the bag and shoved it into her arms. "Why waste time waiting around when we already have a seamstress in the family?"

Still stunned, Sandra could only blink. She wasn't sure what stung more, her mother's disloyalty or her dad's total disregard.

"I…I'm not a seamstress, Dad," she stammered, staring down at the offending bag. "I'm a designer."

"Bottom line is you can sew, right?"

Sewing was something she rarely had time to do as

Swoon continued to grow, and she contracted three expert seamstresses to handle the task.

"Of course I can, but—"

"Good." Her father nodded once, in his view making it a done deal. He glanced down at his wife. "Do you want me to drop you off at home or are you staying to visit?"

Nancy looked from her husband to her daughter. "I'd love to stay and chat a bit, but I need to order Thanksgiving dinner."

"Why? Isn't Milly cooking?" Sandra asked.

Her mother shook her head. "Milly's taking Thanksgiving week off to visit with her grandchildren. I'd cook myself, but I'm committed to spending Thanksgiving morning delivering boxes of groceries for my sorority's needy families program, and the early afternoon helping serve dinners at the church. I simply don't have time to prepare a turkey dinner with all the trimmings." She sighed. "I'll need to order a pie from Carrie at the bakery, too."

"But it isn't even Halloween yet," Sandra said, disappointed that her parents' longtime cook and housekeeper wouldn't be preparing a turkey basted in the sage butter she loved.

"In terms of Thanksgiving in Wintersage, it's already too late. The two best chefs in town aren't taking any more orders, so finding someone to prepare a good meal won't be easy."

A snort came from her father's direction. "Too bad I didn't manage to finagle an invitation from Fred King for Thanksgiving dinner." He turned to Sandra. "Did I mention Ivy prepared a five-course meal while we were there? It was superb."

Sandra pressed her lips together. She loved her Dad, but today he was bouncing on her last nerve like a kid on a trampoline.

Ever since she'd returned home from college and refused to come to work at Woolcott Industries, he'd constantly compared her to the Kings' daughter. The digs had become even more frequent since Ivy had married an executive from her father's company.

Ivy was perfection in the daughter department, while Sandra had descended from Daddy's girl to a big disappointment in her father's eyes. Nothing she did pleased him. All they seemed to do was butt heads.

"Ivy's dinner tasted like it came out of a Michelin starred restaurant. I thought I'd died and gone to heaven with every mouthful," Stuart continued. "And that pie!"

Sandra bit the inside of her lip, hoping her mother would shut him down again.

Instead, Nancy licked her lips. "Which one? The salted caramel chocolate pecan pie or maple bourbon sweet potato pie? Goodness, they both practically melted in your mouth, didn't they?"

"The entire meal did. And to think Ivy made everything from scratch, after putting in a full day helping run their *family business*." Stuart leveled his gaze at Sandra.

"I run a business, too, Dad," Sandra countered, although she knew it wouldn't matter. "I love what I do, and I'm very good at it."

He shook his head. "This isn't about loving what you do, it's about living up to your potential. When you were in school, I'd brag on you to Fred King every time you brought home your grades. He'd be so envious. Now he's the one boasting about how *his daughter's* efforts have resulted in record profits for their business. Not to mention she's also a wife and mother." He exhaled. "Guess who's the jealous father now."

Sandra swallowed the lump rising in her throat. She could show him statements proving Swoon Couture had also raked in sizable profits. She could also reveal, depending on the outcome of next week's election, that she was in the running to design the inaugural ball gown for the wife of Massachusetts's next governor-elect.

But she didn't.

Sandra already knew he wouldn't be impressed *or* proud.

Besides, she'd had enough of family for today. At this point, her best course of action was to get rid of them. *Now.*

"Well, I know you two were eager to be going," she said, mentally shoving them toward her front door. "I'll take care of the dress alterations."

Her parents didn't budge. They were apparently still too overwhelmed by Ivy's cooking to take the hint.

"She doesn't even bother with recipes. Just uses a pinch of this and a little of that," Nancy said.

"That girl's amazing," Stuart exclaimed. "The Kings definitely don't have to be concerned about their holiday dinner, because *their daughter* can do it all."

Sandra's fingers dug into the garment bag still in her arms. She kept her lips pressed together in a firm line as her father smacked his lips loudly.

"Just thinking about what Ivy could do with a turkey, stuffing and all the trimmings sets my mouth to watering," he said.

"Actually, she mentioned jerk turkey was on the menu for Thanksgiving," Nancy added.

Sandra stifled a grunt, along with an overwhelming wave of jealously, which was ridiculous. So what if the Kings' daughter was a great cook, and Sandra wasn't?

It had nothing to do with her. She had nothing to prove.

Then why did she feel that it had everything to do with her, and she had everything to prove?

Stuart raised a questioning brow at his wife. "I could try to wrangle us an invitation to the Kings' Thanksgiving table. It would be terribly pushy, but worth it."

Nancy shook her head. "We can't do that. What about the rest of our family? I'll get to work ordering our holiday dinner as soon as I get home. It won't be Ivy's jerk turkey, but…"

Just when Sandra thought the sensible adult in her had reined in her jealousy, the green-eyed monster inside her broke rank.

"I'll cook," she blurted out.

"What did you say, sweetheart?" her mother asked.

The words continued to bubble out of her mouth of their own accord. "We can have Thanksgiving at my house this year," she said. "I'll do the cooking."

Two pairs of surprised eyes swung toward her. Sandra was sure her own eyes reflected surprise, as well.

"You're kidding, right?" Her father howled with laughter.

When the laughing subsided, he brushed at the tear rolling down his cheek and rested his arm on her shoulder. "Thanks, anyway, but none of us wants to spend the holiday doubled over in the bathroom, or even worse, getting a visit from the fire department."

He burst into another laughing fit, while a giggle her mother had apparently been holding back escaped.

Sandra tried not to feel insulted. Admittedly, she did have a track record in the kitchen that indeed made her offer laughable.

If she was completely honest with herself, she wasn't a cook. She didn't even own a pot or pan. Breakfast was usually coffee and a granola bar. Lunch consisted of a gourmet cupcake from the bakery and dinner was either a hastily eaten deli sandwich or salad in her boutique's studio.

"Don't pay us any mind," her mother said, with a wave of her hand. "It's just, you and the kitchen…"

"Are a match made in hell," her father finished.

Sandra looked on as her parents collapsed into yet another bout of laughter. Increasingly irksome laughter that would have made a less tolerant daughter boot them the heck out of her house.

Instead, Sandra cleared her throat. She'd show her father she was no joke and that there was a lot in her for him to take pride in—starting with Thanksgiving dinner.

"I've got our holiday meal covered," she said firmly, "including a delicious jerking turkey."

"That's jerk turkey," her mother corrected.

"Regardless, I'll expect you two, along with our entire family, here on Thanksgiving Day, ready to eat."

Then she made a mental note to figure out what exactly she had to do to make a turkey *jerk*.

Chapter 2

"I know, Dad," Isaiah Jacobs answered for the umpteenth time.

His old man was spoiling for a fight, but he wouldn't get it. Not today. No matter how hard he tried. Not with the news Isaiah had been blindsided by just two days ago still sinking in.

Isaiah tightened his grip on the old Ford pickup's steering wheel and navigated the winding state road leading back to Wintersage. He was barely a week into civilian life, but tension stiffened his posture as if he was awaiting a fleet admiral's inspection.

"I don't need you hauling me around like a soccer mom, either," Ben Jacobs groused. "I drove myself back and forth for six weeks of treatments. I can certainly do it this last week."

"I know, but I'm here now, and I want to drive you."

Isaiah's conciliatory tone belied the fact that he hadn't given his father a choice in the matter. He'd parked the old pickup, which he'd driven back in high school, crossways, blocking the door to his parents' four-car garage.

"It's bad enough your mother's got me on this god-awful macrobiotic diet. She also banned me from my own office. Threw the fact it's technically *her* family's business in my face and dismissed me like some grunt. After all these years."

Isaiah glanced at the passenger's seat. His father's arms were crossed over his chest and weight loss had made the mulish set to his jaw more pronounced.

"Mom's trying to look out for you," Isaiah said. "And as far as work goes she just insisted you take sick leave. Like she would have done with any Martine's employee in your situation."

"I'm not *any employee*." The elder Jacobs's thunderous baritone rattled the windows of Isaiah's old truck. "I'm president of that damn company."

A president who had been outranked by Martine's Fine Furnishings' worried chairwoman, Cecily Martine Jacobs, who'd resorted to a power play to force her husband to make his health a number-one priority.

"Mom's doing what she thinks is best to—" Isaiah began.

"Don't need mothering or smothering," his father interrupted. "I'm not some kid. I'm a grown man."

So am I. The words sat unspoken on the tip of Isaiah's tongue.

The logical part of him understood his folks' reasoning for not revealing his father's status as soon as they'd found out, camouflaging it in every email, phone call and Skype chat. They hadn't wanted to worry him.

However, the son in him wished he'd been told immediately that his father had been diagnosed with prostate cancer two months ago. Instead of being blindsided by the news his first day home in three years.

"Don't need you patronizing me, either," Ben groused. "We may have the same military rank, *Lieutenant*, but I'm still the parent here."

Keeping his eyes on the road, Isaiah stuck with the same noncombatant phrase he'd repeated all afternoon.

"I know, Dad."

His mother had warned him that while the course of radiation therapy wasn't painful, it had left his father fatigued and ornery.

"And we should have taken my Benz instead of your old truck," his father added. "When was the last time this beater was taken through a car wash, anyway? The neighbors are going to think I've hitched a ride with some backwoods hillbilly, instead of a decorated navy lieutenant."

"*Retired* lieutenant," Isaiah corrected.

A harrumph came from the passenger's seat. "Who the hell retires at twenty-nine years old?"

I do, Isaiah thought.

Like his father and grandfather, he'd gone from Wintersage Academy to the U.S. Naval Academy in Annapolis. Isaiah had graduated a commissioned officer and dedicated the next seven years of his life to the navy, proudly serving his country.

Now, for the first time in over a decade, he was a free man. No longer weighed down by tradition, expectations or duty, he was finally going to follow his own life plan and fulfill his long-held dreams.

Ambitions he hadn't shared with anyone.

Actually, there was one person who knew, he thought. They'd even made plans to pursue their goals, *together*.

But that was a lifetime ago.

Before he could banish it, a faint recollection of a teenage girl with deep chocolate skin and a long raven mane swept up in a high ponytail popped into his head.

Sandra Woolcott.

Isaiah felt the corner of his mouth quirk upward in a half smile at the sweet memory of the first girl to claim his heart. He'd driven along this same road, in this same truck, with a brand-new driver's license in his pocket and Sandra in the passenger's seat.

He could almost hear her laughter as the wind freed her hair from her ponytail and her hair whipped around her face that long-ago spring day.

Isaiah had traveled the world and dated his fair share of women, but he'd yet to come across one more beautiful than Sandra.

Curiosity replaced his musings, and he wondered how her life had turned out. Had she pursued their big plans on her own, after he'd put family expectations and tradition ahead of his own desires and her?

"Hey!" His father's strident tone jarred him out of his reverie. "Have you been gone so long you forgot your way home? You were supposed to make a left at the intersection."

"I know, Dad."

Staring through the windshield at the gray skies, and trees nearing the end of their autumn peak, Isaiah banished thoughts of Sandra to the back of his mind, chalking up the out-of-the-blue flashback to being back in Wintersage.

Ben heaved a drawn-out sigh. The one he used when he was on the brink of losing his patience. "Son, if you say 'I know, Dad' to me one more time…" His father's voice trailed off.

"Sorry," Isaiah said.

"Well, aren't you going to turn this heap around?" Ben groused. "Or do I have to drive us home."

Isaiah shook his head. "We're not going home yet. So just sit tight."

"We're headed downtown?" Ben asked after Isaiah made a left turn.

He nodded, bracing himself for inevitable blowback.

"For what? To give the town busybodies something else to gossip about?" his father protested. "'Poor Ben Jacobs. He looks like a scrawny chicken,'" he mimicked. "Then they sanction their tongue wagging by tacking the words *bless his heart* on the end of every juicy tidbit."

"You may have lost a few pounds, but you look fine," Isaiah said.

His father rested his chin on his chest. "I have my pride, son," he said finally. The volume of his usual booming baritone was so low Isaiah strained to hear.

He swallowed hard, pushing a lump of emotion down his throat, and along with it the urge to turn his truck around and take his dad home.

"Give me ten minutes. After that if you still want to go home, I'll be more than happy to drive you."

Isaiah slowed the truck to the lower posted speed limit as they approached the downtown area near the waterfront. Main Street, usually bustling with tourists and traffic during summer and early autumn, unfurled before him, with only a few residents walking along it.

As his father appeared to be mulling over his offer, Isaiah continued, "Life is short for all of us. Don't let something as trite as pride keep you from enjoying every moment."

He caught his dad's nod in his peripheral vision as he pulled the pickup into an open parking space in front of the bakery. The place had changed ownership in the years he'd been away. A purple awning hung over the storefront window, which boasted a red, white and blue placard asking citizens to vote Oliver Windom to the state house of representatives in the upcoming election.

Both of his parents had raved about the new baker in their emails. His mother was partial to the cinnamon rolls, while his father was wild for the cupcakes. Their enthusiastic reviews had Isaiah raring to try one.

He climbed out of the truck. His first instinct was to go around to the passenger side and help his father, but he decided not to push his luck. Instead, he leaned into the cab.

"Coming?" he asked.

"But what about your mother and that miserable diet?"

"You telling her about this?"

A blast of cold wind and the aroma of cinnamon-laced baked goods wafted through the truck's open door. His father's nose twitched.

"No. I don't think I'll mention it to her, son."

"Good," Isaiah said. "Neither will I."

Ben bounded from the truck with more energy than Isaiah had seen in the few days he'd been back. His father stopped short at the bakery door. He frowned, and then grunted at the sign in the window. "I wouldn't vote to elect Windom dogcatcher," he grumbled.

A rush of heat and more heavenly smells greeted them inside the bakery. Isaiah's stomach rumbled, reminding him he'd only picked at his breakfast and skipped lunch altogether.

"Ben!" A woman clad in a purple apron with the bakery's logo etched on the front greeted his father with a warm smile. "Long time no see. Where have you been keeping yourself?"

His father mumbled something about being busy, not quite meeting the woman's eyes.

"Well, it's good to see you. I thought I'd lost one of my best customers to some cockamamy low-carb diet." She turned to Isaiah. "And this must be the son you've told me about, because he looks just like you."

His father perked up, any self-consciousness pushed aside by his deprived sweet tooth and the array of cupcakes on display behind the glass case. He briefly introduced Isaiah to the middle-aged woman called Carrie, before the two launched into a discussion about her latest culinary creations.

"I know you're partial to the red velvet." Carrie held up a cupcake heaped with white frosting and red sprinkles. "But you've got to try my new salted caramel and corn candy cupcakes."

Ben pressed a finger against his lips as he glanced from the cupcake in her hand to the ones in the display.

"I'm only baking the corn candy ones until Halloween, on Friday. After that they won't return until next year," she coaxed.

"I'll take two of the corn candy," Isaiah said, not sharing his father's indecisiveness.

Carrie put two cupcakes smothered in orange icing and topped with corn candy on a purple plate. Isaiah's stomach rumbled again as she placed them on the counter.

"Okay, give me one of the salted caramel," his father finally said.

"One?" Carrie raised a brow. Ignoring his request, she placed two of the oversize cakes on a purple plate and handed it to Ben.

Isaiah retrieved his wallet from his back pocket and pulled out a twenty to pay.

Carrie shook her head, refusing it. "It's on the house. Thank you for your service, son." She glanced briefly at his father and back at him, understanding brimming in her warm brown eyes. "And for bringing one of my favorite customers back."

Isaiah nodded and returned his wallet to his pocket.

"Have a seat," she continued. "I'm brewing a fresh pot of coffee. I'll bring some over when it's done."

He retrieved his cupcakes and followed his father. After his old man's initial reluctance to even step inside the bakery, Isaiah was surprised to see him select a table by the window, overlooking the town's main thoroughfare.

Not bothering with preliminaries, they immediately took huge bites out of the tower of creamy icing covering their confections.

One mouthful and Isaiah knew why his father was hooked. The rich, sugary rush of flavor was addictive.

"Mmm." Ben closed his eyes briefly and sighed. "Is this not the best thing you ever tasted?"

His own mouth stuffed with another huge bite, Isaiah could only nod.

Neither man looked up from his plate until Carrie returned with coffee and a purple box with the bakery's logo.

"I wrapped up a cinnamon roll for Cecily." She glanced down at their nearly empty plates and winked. "You two make sure she gets it."

After Carrie left, Isaiah sipped his coffee and looked at his father, who was staring out the window. His face still bore the fine lines of weariness, but he sat a little straighter and the pastry appeared to have elevated his mood.

Ben took a sip of coffee. "Thanks for bringing me here," he said, continuing to gaze out at the passing cars and occasional pedestrian. "Sorry I gave you a hard time."

"No big deal."

The sun made a sudden appearance, poking through the blanket of gray clouds dominating the skies. His father squinted against the beams streaming through the storefront window.

"We can move to another table," Isaiah offered.

"No, it's cool." Ben faced the sun. "Other than driving back and forth to Boston for my treatments, I've been holed up at the house."

Isaiah figured as much. It was why he'd insisted on bringing him here.

His father turned away from the window. Wrapping his hands around his coffee mug, he looked down at the still-steaming brew before focusing his attention on Isaiah. "You haven't said what your plans are now that you're out of the military," he said. "I don't suppose they include staying in Wintersage permanently."

They didn't. He'd intended to spend only the next

month with his folks. The day after Thanksgiving, he was booked on a flight bound for London.

He shook his head. Although his father's prognosis was excellent, the cancer diagnosis had shaken Isaiah. He didn't want to think about leaving. Not yet. Not until after his father completed his course of radiation therapy this week, and they'd gotten a follow-up report from his doctors.

"I'm here now," he said.

Ben smiled, sunlight washing over his drawn face.

"Then how about doing your old dad a favor?"

"Sure. What do you need?"

His father rubbed a hand over the stubble along his chin.

"As you know, Martine's Fine Furnishings still sponsors the children's Halloween party at the recreation center. This year, I'd like you to stand in for me and your mother."

The tradition had started with Isaiah's maternal great-grandfather, a Halloween night nearly a half century ago, when the town's residents had taken shelter in the basement of the recreation center as a late-season hurricane battered the Massachusetts shoreline. It went on to become an annual event and a Wintersage institution.

Isaiah speculated that his father was more exhausted than he'd let on if he'd consider missing it.

"No problem. You just take it easy and rest up for next year." Isaiah drained the last of the coffee in his mug with one gulp.

"Rest?" Ben laughed. "I can rest when I'm dead."

"I don't understand."

"I've been sitting here thinking about what you said

about life being short. Cancer has hung over me like a dark cloud the past few months. Even before my diagnosis, life for your mother and I revolved around the company," he said. "I can't think of the last time either of us has done anything unrelated to the company and now illness."

Isaiah listened as his father continued.

"I plan to remedy that. Starting this Friday with Halloween," Ben said. "My last radiation treatment is Friday morning. Afterward, I'm going to persuade your mother to take off work and spend the day in Salem for some good, scary fun. We can take one of those corny ghost tours, visit the House of the Seven Gables and the Salem Witch Museum and then spend the night at a local bed-and-breakfast."

Isaiah couldn't help wondering if his father was moving too fast. Four more days of treatments would leave him more fatigued than he was now.

Isaiah looked down at his empty coffee mug and searched his brain for a diplomatic way of saying so without offending him.

"Our first date was on Halloween, you know," his father said. "I took her to see one of those gory slasher films that were all the rage back then. Somewhere between the on-screen screams and Cecily spilling an entire tub of popcorn on me, I fell in love."

His father's reminiscence caught Isaiah off guard. It was the first time he had heard that story.

While Isaiah was growing up, Ben's references to the past had focused exclusively on stories of the Jacobs men who'd come before him, and Isaiah's duty to follow in their footsteps to Annapolis and then the navy.

Isaiah credited the uncharacteristic sentimental recollection to the cancer diagnosis.

"Perhaps you should give your body a little recovery time before playing tourist and considering an overnighter. Who knows how you'll feel come Friday?"

Ben opened the box Carrie had left on the table, pulled out the cinnamon roll earmarked for his wife, and took a bite out of it. He appeared to mull over Isaiah's concerns as he chewed. "Salem's right down the road, and a shorter drive from here than Boston. If I get tired, we'll check into the bed-and-breakfast early."

"How about renting a scary movie and chilling out at home?" Isaiah suggested.

"I'm not asking your permission, son. All I'm asking is for you to stand in for us at an event sponsored by our family business." Picking up a napkin, Ben wiped white icing from his fingertips. "Will you do that for me?"

Isaiah nodded.

He wanted to spend his short time in Wintersage helping his folks, and if that meant playing host at a children's party, so be it.

Chapter 3

Why couldn't she have just kept her mouth shut?

Sandra walked the short blocks to The Quarterdeck restaurant in a zombielike stupor.

Autumn was her favorite season. Yet she couldn't appreciate the scent of firewood permeating the crisp night air or the wind rustling the few leaves still clinging to trees. The jack-o'-lanterns and campaign placards in the shop windows she passed were a blur.

Reality had set in, and all she could think about was the big fat Thanksgiving mess she'd gotten herself into. Thanks to a childish need to constantly prove herself to her dad.

She yanked open the door to the restaurant and blinked as she walked inside.

The usual elegant ambience of her Monday night haunt had undergone a transformation since last week.

Paper lanterns adorned with bats and witches riding brooms hung from the rafters, while faux cobwebs, plastic skeletons and gravestones held up the corners of the restaurant's spacious dining room.

Sandra gulped. First Halloween, then before you knew it, Thanksgiving would be upon them.

Looking up at a witch silhouetted on one of the paper lanterns, she briefly wondered if it could cast a spell that would give her Martha Stewart's kitchen skills in less than a month.

Sandra sighed. Probably not.

She scanned the room and easily spotted her friend seated at a table near the bar. The old-fashioned, school-marm bun Vicki Ahlfors kept her long hair swept up in had given her away.

Sandra smiled, the sight of her friend buoying her sagging spirits.

"Sorry I'm late." She leaned over and gave her a quick hug.

"Where have you been hiding all day?" Vicki asked. "I came upstairs to see if you were free for lunch, but the lights in your studio were off and the door was locked."

Best friends since high school, Sandra, Vicki and Janelle Howerton were also business partners. The trio ran their complementary businesses out of a three-story Victorian located a block from Main Street.

Vicki's flower shop, Petals, occupied the first floor, Sandra's Swoon Couture was on the second, while Janelle operated her events planning business, Alluring Affairs, from the top floor. The arrangement had been profitable as well as convenient, and the three of them often collaborated on some of the town's splashiest weddings and social functions.

"I worked from home today." Sandra plopped down at the table across from her. "Then my folks stopped over."

Vicki frowned. "But I thought they went to New York City right after Janelle's wedding to visit friends."

Sandra's gaze flicked to the empty chair at their table, before turning to the waiter who'd come to take her drink order.

"White wine?" the college kid who often waited tables on Monday nights guessed.

Sandra looked across at Vicki's white wine spritzer. She automatically nodded, but changed her mind. She definitely needed something stronger this evening.

"On second thought…" She picked up the drinks menu. Within moments she'd narrowed down her choices to either a manhattan or a red apple cidertini.

"It's not on the menu, but this week's special is a pumpkin martini," the waiter suggested.

"Sounds great," Sandra said. "I'll take it."

When he'd left to retrieve the drink, Sandra noticed her friend eyeing her suspiciously.

"What did your dad say this time?" Vicki asked.

Sandra's mouth dropped open. "How'd you know he…"

"The combination of your folks dropping by unexpectedly and you ordering a cocktail make it obvious," she said. "So what did he do? Call your sketch pad a coloring book again? Complain you were rotting your brilliant brain playing paper dolls and dress up?"

"Doesn't matter what he said now," Sandra said. "I'm the problem. Me and my big mouth."

She quickly filled her friend in on her parents' visit, from them dumping another designer's dresses on her to alter, to her father's nonstop praise of his friend's superdaughter, and finally Sandra's big, dumb Thanksgiving offer.

Vicki's eyes widened to the size of Ping-Pong balls.

"But…" her friend began. The horrified look on her face matched the restaurant's scary decor.

Their waiter returned with Sandra's martini. When he left, Vicki leaned across the table. "I know your dad can sometimes be a bit much, but what on earth possessed you to say such a thing?" she asked. "You can't cook."

"That's an understatement." Sandra took a tentative sip of her drink, the syrupy sweetness of pumpkin and maple syrup disguising the vodka's kick.

"Remember when you baked chocolate chip cookies for the cheerleader fund-raiser?"

Sandra rolled her eyes skyward and snorted. "Don't remind me. I think my dad is still getting dental bills from people biting down on those hockey pucks."

The waiter reappeared to take their dinner orders. Again, Sandra opted for one of the restaurant's Halloween specials, pumpkin ravioli in a lobster cream sauce, while her friend ordered the broiled haddock.

"So what are you going to do?" Vicki asked after the waiter left.

Sandra sighed. "The way I see it, I only have two options. Either tell my folks I misspoke, or buy myself a cookbook, a set of pots and pans and start practicing. I could do a trial run with a small dinner party with you, Janelle and Ballard."

"Oh, no. I'm not playing guinea pig." Vicki put her

hand up and shook her head. "And I'm sure Janelle isn't going to subject her new husband's stomach to your kitchen experiments."

Again, Sandra glanced at the empty chair. "But you're my best friends, and I need you," she said, her tone a mixture of whining and pleading. "We're *The Silk Sisters*, remember?"

She'd hoped tossing out their old high school nickname, now the name of the corporation the trio had formed with their businesses, would soften Vicki's stance.

Instead, the florist frowned. "As your best friend, I'd suggest you swallow your pride, go crawling to your dad and beg off cooking Thanksgiving dinner." She took a sip of wine. "Or for that matter, *any* meal."

Sandra took an unladylike gulp from her own drink. "Crawl and beg, huh?"

Vicki nodded once. "Exactly."

Fifteen minutes later, their waiter slid hot plates bearing their dinner in front of them. Sandra gazed down at her food. It looked and smelled delicious, but all she could think about was the smug expression on her father's face when she reneged after insisting she'd cook.

"I know you're right." Sandra sighed. "But my dad would never let me hear the end of it. He'll be ribbing me until New Year's."

Vicki speared a piece of fish with her fork. "Better than your entire family spending Thanksgiving in the bathroom, at the dentist or even worse, the emergency room at Wintersage Hospital."

Sandra opened her mouth to protest, but knew she didn't have a case. Instead, she helped herself to a mouthful of ravioli.

"Okay, I'll call off the bet," she said, having decided to see her parents first thing tomorrow morning and cancel plans to have Thanksgiving at her place. "So what's going on with you, besides being inundated with orders for fall harvest floral arrangements?"

Vicki looked up from her plate. "Planning my parade float for the annual Wintersage Christmas Celebration. I know it's a while away, but I still have so much to do. I got sidetracked helping with Janelle's wedding."

"Same here," Sandra agreed. "But it was a beautiful wedding. I don't think I've ever seen her so happy."

This time they both cast a glance at the empty chair at their table. Sandra wasn't sure how long she stared at the seat that usually would have been occupied by their friend.

"Janelle didn't leave town for good, you know," Vicki said. "She's just on her honeymoon. She'll be back next week, in time for the election."

"Yeah, I know." Sandra shrugged.

No way would Janelle miss the election, not with her father running against Oliver Windom in the most talked about race in the state.

"Then why that face?"

Sandra didn't need a mirror to know she looked as if she'd lost her best friend, because no matter how Vicki put it, the reality was she had. While Vicki hadn't come on the scene until she transferred from the local public high school to Wintersage Academy in the tenth grade, Sandra and Janelle had been friends since kindergarten.

"Don't get me wrong, I'm thrilled for Janelle," Sandra explained. "Yet the selfish part of me is a little sad, because things won't be the same once she and Ballard return from Tahiti."

The waiter cleared their empty plates and rattled off the dessert offerings. They ordered a second round of drinks, and a slice of cheesecake to share.

Vicki stared at her nearly empty wineglass. "I was thinking about it earlier at the shop. You're right. It won't be the same. Janelle is a happily married woman now, and we're single. It's a different mind-set."

Sandra nodded. "Her life will revolve around her husband, and before you know it, the babies will start coming…" If their friend didn't return home from her honeymoon already pregnant, she thought, downing the last of her first martini.

"Well, hopefully, love, weddings and lots of babies are in our futures, too." Vicki's tone softened along with her gaze. "Sooner rather than later."

Sandra coughed, nearly choking on her drink.

"S-speak for yourself," she sputtered. "I'm not in the market for a husband, and my nephew is enough baby for me."

"Oh, come on. Aren't you tired of having no one to come home to at the end of a long, hard day?"

"Nope, it's why I moved out of my parents' house and into one of my own as soon as Swoon became profitable."

The waiter returned bearing their drinks and dessert. Sandra immediately reached for the fresh cocktail, its sugary rush reminiscent of a milk shake. However, if she thought the decadent slab of New York cheesecake at the center of the table was going to dissuade her friend from pursuing the current topic of conversation, she was mistaken.

"Well, aren't you sick of wasting your time on meaningless dates with guys you know would never make the cut for Mr. Right?"

"Nope. At twenty-eight years old, it's called being young and having fun. In fact, I have a date Friday night with a cute Mr. Let's-Just-Have-a-Good-Time lawyer. We're going to a Halloween party in Boston."

Vicki sighed. "I'm all for fun and good times, but I want to start having them with a special someone. Janelle already has her Prince Charming. I'm ready for mine and my happily-ever-after."

"Not me. I have goals to achieve." Sandra picked up one of the two forks that had accompanied the cheesecake. "They don't include being sidetracked by a needy Prince Charming and a drudgery-filled, so-called happily-ever-after spent catering to him."

She shoved a forkful of cheesecake into her mouth.

Already a die-hard romantic, Vicki was simply swept up in the romance of Janelle's wedding, Sandra thought. No wedding, or for that matter, no *man* was going to sway her from her dream of taking Swoon Couture beyond Wintersage.

If next week's election went the way she hoped, and her design was selected by the governor-elect's wife, it would garner her design business statewide, perhaps even national, attention.

Vicki dug into the cheesecake with her fork. "A man who's truly your Prince Charming won't divert you from your goals. He'll want to be there to cheer you on as you achieve them."

Sandra rolled her eyes. "Maybe in fairy-tale land, where Mr. Right and Prince Charming reside, along with the fictitious Knight in Shining Armor."

Her friend helped herself to another bite of cheese-cake, staring at her as she chewed. "If you say so," she said.

"I do."

Vicki shrugged. "Back in the day, I'd have bet money you would have been the first one of us to say 'I do' and start living a happily-ever-after, with your high school sweetheart."

Isaiah.

After years of not giving him much thought, Sandra found his name popping into her head for the second time that day. Again, images of the tall athletic boy with the dreamy eyes washed over her. They'd been so in love and had made so many plans for the future.

Plans that years later seemed as absurd as the notion of her cooking Thanksgiving dinner.

"That was a long time ago, and we were just kids," Sandra said.

"Yeah, but you two seemed so perfect for each other. Do you ever wonder how things would have turned out if Isaiah hadn't left?"

For the entire summer after he'd gone to the naval academy, Sandra had stayed awake nights asking the same question. *What if...* But back then she'd been a naive seventeen-year-old girl who hadn't known squat about real life.

"Isaiah was just a high school sweetheart, who I haven't seen since he left Wintersage," she said. "I think about him as much as I do Mrs. Sterling's chemistry class or after-school cheerleader practice, which is never."

Sandra took a sip of the sweet martini. Isaiah's mother, Cecily, was one of her private clients, but she hadn't seen much of her lately. When she did come into the boutique, neither of them brought up the subject of her son.

Isaiah had come home to see his parents from time to time over the years, however Sandra hadn't run into him during those brief visits.

Vicki exhaled, one of those drawn-out, dreamy, love-conquers-all sighs. "After all these years, I still remember the way he used to look at you," she said, "like you were the most beautiful girl he'd ever seen."

Sandra rolled her eyes again. It was time to shut down the subject, otherwise her friend would continue on the path of blowing a long-ago adolescent infatuation totally out of proportion.

"I'm sure Isaiah Jacobs is somewhere on the other side of the world, with his choice of beautiful women," she said, picking up her fork again to dig into the dwindling slice of cheesecake.

"You're probably right," Vicki agreed.

"So my brainpower would be better utilized thinking about the here and the now, like how I'm going to catch up on a backlog of work and get out of turning Thanksgiving into a fiasco."

Her friend scrunched up her nose. "Especially the part about Thanksgiving."

Sandra laughed and reached for her drink. Then a man standing at the dining room entrance caught her eye, and she froze, martini poised in midair.

The shoulders beneath the leather bomber jacket were broader, the once lanky body packed with lean muscle, but it was his face, those familiar eyes.

Isaiah.

It couldn't be. Sandra blinked, and whoever she'd thought she had seen vanished.

"What's the matter with you?" Vicki asked. "You look like you saw a Halloween ghost."

"It was nothing." She put her martini down and picked up her water glass instead.

She'd obviously already had more than enough to drink. Too much alcohol, the spooky Halloween ambience and out-of-the-blue thoughts of Isaiah today had wreaked havoc on her imagination.

They'd simply stirred up the devil, that's all. The sexy devil who'd broken her teenage heart.

One glimpse confirmed it.

After all these years, Sandra Woolcott was still the most beautiful woman Isaiah had ever seen.

He'd left before she'd noticed him standing at the entrance of the restaurant's dining room, watching her.

Spellbound.

Drinking in her familiar, yet now mature, features like a man who'd stumbled across an oasis after walking the desert for days.

Isaiah slowed his truck at the entrance of Martine's Fine Furnishings' headquarters and punched a pass code into the keypad to open the gate. His plan had been to sidestep another one of the macrobiotic meals his mother had delivered to the house daily. Tonight's entrée, a corn-and-bean casserole, held little appeal.

He'd craved steak and figured The Quarterdeck still served the best in town. But instead of the satisfying meal he'd anticipated, Isaiah had left the restaurant with an altogether different craving. An overwhelming longing for the girl he thought he'd gotten over a decade ago.

And he had gotten over her, he reminded himself, as images of Sandra throwing back her head and laughing at something her longtime friend Vicki had said played through his mind. A laugh that reached her eyes and illuminated her entire face.

He used to make her laugh like that, he thought. Back then the pitch of her laughter was higher, giggle-infused and incredibly sweet.

Tonight, it had been softer, and held a husky note he found incredibly sexy.

Isaiah drove the truck past the three-story office building that housed Martine's business and design centers. He stayed on the path that wound through the complex, driving past the huge warehouse from which they shipped furniture ordered at any of their fifteen showrooms, located throughout Massachusetts, Maine and New Hampshire.

He shifted the truck's gear stick into Park next to a storage shed that had been the company's original warehouse when it opened for business seventy-five years ago. No matter how many times they'd painted the old shed red, it didn't stay that way long. Within a year the combination of salty ocean air, summer sun and harsh winter nor'easters turned the wood back to a weather-beaten gray.

Using the same key code he'd punched in at the gate, Isaiah waited for the electronic lock to click before pulling open the shed's wide double doors and turning on the fluorescent overhead lights.

It was odd being out here without his father by his side giving orders.

Ben had always set up the children's games for the recreation center Halloween party personally, saying it gave him an opportunity to get out from behind his desk. They'd done it together when Isaiah was growing up.

Surprisingly, his old man hadn't protested when Isaiah had volunteered to do it alone this year. They both knew the radiation treatments had sapped the stamina needed to lift the heavy wooden props used for most of the games.

Since the unexpected Sandra sighting had vanquished his hunger, Isaiah decided to dig the games out of storage and check their condition tonight before hauling them over to the recreation center Friday. The physical labor would reignite his appetite and give him something to do besides dwell on a woman he no longer knew.

Still, he couldn't help but wonder.

Had Sandra gone through with the plans they'd made together, after he'd left for Annapolis? Had she spent that summer in Chicago attending the prestigious School of the Art Institute's early college program? Did she study fashion design there after graduating Wintersage Academy?

Isaiah shook his head, as if the gesture could shake off the onslaught of memories and questions that seeing her again dredged up.

"Whatever Sandra Woolcott did then or is up to now is none of your business," he muttered.

Easily locating the games in the same corner of the dusty shed they'd always occupied, awaiting their annual Halloween appearance, Isaiah pulled work gloves from his back pocket. He lifted the two six-foot wooden panels used for the giant beanbag tosses from the floor, and leaned them against the wall. One was in the shape of a giant pumpkin and the other a giant tricolor corn candy.

Both looked shabby. Their once bright orange paint had either faded, peeled or chipped away.

Isaiah sighed. It was a good thing he'd made a trip over here before Friday. These definitely needed work, and he suspected the rest would, too.

He walked back to his truck to grab his phone, planning to make a list of things he'd need to get them looking festive again. He opened the driver's side door, leaned inside the cab and opened the armrest compartment. He paused at the sound of his name.

"Is that you?" a voice called out in the darkness.

Isaiah straightened and watched a tall, heavy-set man approach. As he got closer the lights illuminating the complex revealed a round, vaguely familiar face.

"Hey, it is you." The man's eyes brightened. He slapped him on the back as Isaiah struggled to place him. "When did you get back into town?"

"I got home on Friday." Isaiah's eyes narrowed. "Tony?" he asked, the voice jogging his memory.

"Yeah, it's me." The round face split into a wide grin as he patted a belly threatening to pop the buttons on his jacket. "Me and fifty pounds of my wife's good cooking."

Isaiah laughed and gave his old teammate's hand a vigorous shake. "Great to see you. How've you been, man?" He looked down at his friend's stomach. "Besides well fed."

During Isaiah's stint as quarterback of Wintersage Academy's football team, Anthony Green had been his go-to receiver.

The two of them had been a powerful combination

guaranteed to make big plays and put points on the board. Unfortunately, their efforts were rarely enough to keep pace with the points their team's notoriously weak defense gave up every game.

"I'm good. The wife and I are expecting again, twins this time. Fortunately, I survived the latest round of layoffs here, and your mom recently promoted me to warehouse supervisor."

Layoffs? His parents hadn't mentioned letting employees go. Isaiah made a mental note to ask them about it.

"Congratulations all around," Isaiah said.

"What about you, Lieutenant Jacobs? You on leave?"

"Yup, permanently. I put in my time, and I'm officially an honorably discharged civilian."

"Cool." Tony leaned against Isaiah's truck. "Figured you'd be back sooner or later to take over the company."

Isaiah shook his head. "I'm just visiting with my folks for a couple of weeks."

Retrieving his smartphone from the truck and tucking it in his pocket, Isaiah inclined his head toward the shed. "I came out to check over the games for the children's party at the rec center on Friday. I just got started, but from what I've seen so far they're going to need some work."

"I'll give you a hand." Tony fell in step beside him as he walked back to the shed.

"Are you sure? After all, you have a family at home waiting."

"My mother-in-law's in town. I got off an hour ago, but I'm trying to drag the workday out until she either leaves or goes to bed."

Isaiah laughed at the pained comical expression that crossed his old high school classmate's face.

Inside the shed, Tony wasn't much help. However, he kept Isaiah company with a steady stream of chatter, updating him on happenings in Wintersage.

"Wintersage Academy's football team actually has a shot at making the finals this year," Tony said.

A spider skittered across the gravel floor as Isaiah brushed a coating of cobwebs off another old board with what looked like a black cat painted on it.

"Didn't they manage to win a championship a few years after we graduated?" Isaiah thought he'd read a brief about it in the online edition of the *Boston Herald*.

"They made it to the finals, but lost the championship to Bourne High School."

Isaiah let out a low whistle and shook his head. "Those Bourne High Canelmen were some big boys, weren't they? I remember them sacking me like I was a rag doll."

Tony pinched a chunk of fat above his waist between two fingers. "I feel a twinge in the ribs they bruised every time it rains."

Isaiah chuckled, his smile fading as he looked at the pitiful assortment of Halloween-themed games.

More than worn and faded, they all seemed terribly dated. It made him wonder if they were worth the trouble of salvaging. However, with only three days left until Halloween, he'd have to think of something. Fast.

"Hey, Tony, your kids attend the Halloween party at the rec center, right?"

"Every year." His friend nodded. "Along with every other kid under ten in Wintersage."

"What do they think of it? Do they have a good time?"

Tony averted his eyes and kicked at a pebble with his shoe. "I usually volunteer to help, along with a dozen or so Martine employees."

"Do your kids have a good time?" Isaiah asked again.

"Depends," he said finally. "Am I talking to an old teammate or the boss's son?"

"My folks are Martine's Fine Furnishings. Not me. Speak your mind."

"Well, my toddler liked it okay, but my other two, who were five and seven last year, were only interested in the candy." Tony cast a glance at the boards stacked against the wall. "They said the games were boring, and wanted to leave to go trick-or-treating."

Isaiah couldn't blame his friend's kids for wanting to ditch the party. Now that Tony had mentioned it, he could remember feeling the same way when he was around seven. He'd always attended the party, not just because of his family connection, but because it was what kids in Wintersage did on Halloween.

An idea began to form in his mind as he continued to stare at the antiquated games. He didn't run the family business, but he was the host of this party. It was time to shake things up. Give it a twenty-first century update and make it fun.

Fun.

He turned the word around in his head. Then it hit him. What could be more fun than a fun house?

Excited about a concept he could sink his artistic teeth into, Isaiah pulled his phone from his jacket pocket. First he checked Friday's weather forecast, and then he began making a list of items and people he'd need to turn the recreation center into a Halloween-themed carnival fun house by Friday.

He could make a hardware store run after his father's treatment tomorrow. He'd also stop by the art supply store, where he already had a running list of items he wanted to pick up, including the Conté crayons he liked to use for sketching.

Isaiah hoped to do some drawings of the seacoast at dawn and dusk before he left for London, and perhaps capture the late-autumn beauty of Wintersage's beach in a watercolor if time permitted.

"So have you seen Sandra yet?" Tony asked.

Isaiah froze at the sound of her name. He'd been so caught up in thoughts of sketching on the beach, he'd forgotten Tony was there.

His old teammate took his silence as a memory lapse. "Sandra Woolcott. Don't tell me you've forgotten her. Not as tight as you two were back in school."

No. He'd never forgotten Sandra, Isaiah silently admitted.

"Yeah, I saw her tonight." His outer cool belied the inner mayhem that seeing her again had stirred up.

He kept his eyes glued to the list he'd been making on his phone as his friend continued. "She was cute in high school, but now…" Tony shook his head. "Man, is she hot. And those hourglass curves of hers." He shook his head again. "Mmm, mmm. Thick in all the right places."

Looking up from his phone, Isaiah frowned, ticked off for no good reason. "Don't you have a wife?"

Tony pointed a finger in his direction. "Yeah, and if she gets wind of what I just said you'll be responsible for the bruising of my other ribs."

Isaiah threw his head back and laughed. Just like in high school, his old teammate's good-natured sense of humor made it impossible for anyone to stay annoyed with him long.

Besides, what did he care if Tony checked out Sandra on the sly? She'd been seated when he'd seen her at the restaurant earlier, so he couldn't cosign on his friend's assessment of her figure.

Yet the little he'd seen of her had left an indelible impression. Luminous dark skin, pillow-soft lips and a sultry laugh that shot straight to his groin.

Tony snorted. "If anyone had told me back then that I'd be the married one and you'd still be a bachelor, I wouldn't have believed them. I'd thought for sure you and Sandra would have gotten hitched as soon as she graduated."

His friend had handed him the perfect opening to ask the question buzzing through his mind ever since he'd seen her earlier at The Quarterdeck.

Was she seeing someone? Engaged, or maybe married, with a couple of kids?

She'd looked happy in the restaurant. Radiant.

Reminding himself it was none of his business, Isaiah stuffed his phone back into his jacket pocket. Deep down, he knew he didn't want to hear his friend's answers to the questions. Isaiah didn't want to think of his first love with another man.

An ancient wooden pin from the bowling game fell away from the rest. Isaiah picked it up and tossed it back on the pile.

"We were just kids with a bad case of, what do they call it…" He paused, trying to think of the term, and then snapped his fingers when it came to him. "Yeah, puppy love."

Tony shrugged. "All I know is she had your nose wide open."

"Hardly." The lie rolled off Isaiah's lips as if it were truth.

"Come on, man. I was there," his teammate said. "Remember the time when we were doing our pregame warm-ups, and you spotted Sandra on the sidelines in her cheerleader uniform?"

Isaiah shook his head as he automatically reached to touch an old scar, hidden by his short-cropped hair.

"Uh-huh." Tony looked at Isaiah's hand. "Isn't that the spot where you damn near split your head open after you ran into the goalpost because of gawking at her?"

Busted, Isaiah shoved his traitorous hands into his jacket pockets.

Good thing high school was over, and he never had to worry about seeing Sandra Woolcott in a cheerleader uniform again.

Chapter 4

Three days later, Sandra steered her yellow MINI Cooper with one hand and answered her cell phone with the other.

"Where are you?" Vicki demanded.

"Stopped at a red light, but I'm almost there."

"Good, because the longer you wait, the worse it'll be for you."

"You're right," Sandra grumbled, as she turned off the main thoroughfare onto a familiar private road. She'd been putting off this visit since Tuesday.

Each time she thought about telling her parents she was backing out of cooking on Thanksgiving, she pictured the smug I-told-you-so expression sure to stretch across her father's face, and found another reason to stall.

Sandra slowed the car to a stop in the circular driveway in front of her parents' two-story Colonial and stared through the windshield at the house she'd grown up in. No doubt her folks had eaten dinner by now and adjourned to the den to watch *Jeopardy*.

"I'm here," she said into the phone.

"Go on and get it over with," Vicki coaxed.

"Crawl, beg, retract." Sandra repeated the strategy she'd rehearsed at her friend's flower shop.

"Exactly," Vicki said. "And whatever you do, don't let your dad provoke you into saying something that will get you into even more of a predicament than you're in now."

"Don't worry. I won't."

Sandra ended the call with a promise to check in with her friend after the deed was done. Moments later, she opened her parents' front door and called out her arrival.

Silence.

The ticktock sounds of a game show jingle weren't blaring throughout the house. Nor did she hear her mother shouting answers in the form of a question, while her father insisted to an unhearing Alex Trebek his answers to the quiz show's questions were *not* wrong.

"Mom. Dad," she yelled out again, walking through the living room and down the hallway leading to the family room. She peeked inside.

The large flat-screen television was off and the leather sofa facing it sat empty.

Frowning, Sandra went to the kitchen, where she found her parents' longtime housekeeper, Milly, standing at the kitchen island work space. Earbuds from the iPod Sandra had given her last Christmas were stuffed in her ears and a pen stuck in her hair, which was

twisted into a French braid. The older woman was totally engrossed in her laptop screen and the textbook
opened beside it.

Sandra flicked the kitchen light off and then on again
to avoid startling her.

Yanking the earbuds from her ears, Milly turned
around. She spotted Sandra and smiled. "Hey there,
stranger," she said. "You just missed your brother. He
stopped by to pick up a Halloween costume your mom
bought for little Mason."

"Was the baby with him?" Sandra asked.

"Your mother volunteered to take him to the bedtime
story program at the library, so Jordan could work late
on the Windom campaign," Milly said.

Sandra wasn't surprised her mother had absconded
with the toddler. Both she and Nancy babysat whenever
they could to give Jordan, who had primary custody of
his son, a break. However, between the preparations
for Janelle's hastily arranged wedding and trying to
get caught up at work, Sandra hadn't seen her nephew
in nearly two weeks.

No way was she going to miss seeing him decked
out in his pint-size Patriots uniform.

She had a date tomorrow night, and Jordan's ex-wife
was supposed to pick up Mason for her scheduled visi-
tation. Sandra made a mental note to arrange to see her
nephew before Allison arrived.

Rounding the kitchen island, she peered over Milly's shoulder. "You in an online class session or doing
homework?"

"Homework. Class ended an hour ago."

Having put two children through college, Milly had
begun pursuing her own education after her youngest

graduated from Boston College. Now the fifty-five-year-old cook and housekeeper was only a few credits shy of earning her bachelor's degree in business administration. She already had standing job offers from both Woolcott Industries and Sandra's Swoon Couture.

"Microeconomics?"

Milly nodded. "I've got a quiz to study for and a paper to write. Both are kicking my old behind."

"Need some help?" Sandra offered.

"Not this time, sweetheart. You've already helped me get through my science elective last year, and then Analyzing Financial Statements last semester." She patted Sandra's hand. "Besides, your dad offered to look over the paper when I'm done. It isn't due until December, but I want to get it off my back before I leave for the Thanksgiving holiday. I may want to extend it and spend more time with my grandchildren."

Sandra groaned. The mentions of both her father and the holiday reminded her this visit wasn't exactly a social call.

"Speaking of Thanksgiving," Milly said, "word is you're cooking this year's feast." She scrunched up her nose and shivered. "No offense, but I'm glad I'll be out of town."

An idea popped into Sandra's head. She smiled and put her arm around the older woman. Maybe she wouldn't have to rescind the offer, after all.

"Um…I was thinking maybe you could teach…" Sandra leaned down and placed her head on the housekeeper's shoulder.

"Oh, no." Milly shook her off. "I tried to teach you to cook when you were a little girl, and again as a teenager, remember?"

"But…"

Milly held up two fingers. "Twice I tried. First there was the spaghetti sauce explosion. I scrubbed this kitchen for three hours before giving up, and your father hiring a cleaning crew. And let's not leave out the *stir-fry fire.*"

Sandra wasn't going to let her off that easy. "But I helped you with your classes." She started by pleading, but when she saw she wasn't making any inroads, she changed her approach midstream.

"You owe me, Milly," she said firmly.

Swayed by neither argument, the older woman responded with a humorless chuckle. "Don't even try it with me," she said. "I suggest you march yourself out to the garage, where your father's tinkering with his second wife, and rescind that ludicrous offer to cook."

Sandra felt her shoulders slump. She should have known better than to think she could get something over on Milly. "But you're still coming to work for me at Swoon when you graduate, right?"

"We'll see."

The housekeeper walked over to the big jar on the granite counter near the sink. She retrieved an oatmeal raisin cookie and handed it to Sandra. "Good luck."

Polishing it off, Sandra walked out the back door and cut across the dormant lawn to the garage. She could hear the pounding beat of an eighties rap group coming through the side door as she approached.

She pushed open the door, knowing her dad wouldn't hear a knock over the music.

Stuart, dressed in coveralls to protect the shirt and tie he'd worn to work that day, looked up from under the hood of the Chevelle. He saw her and smiled, a warm smile that made the fine lines around his brown eyes crinkle.

It brought home the fact that no matter how much of a disappointment she might be to him, no matter how much he could annoy her, he was her daddy, and she loved him.

Sandra returned his smile. She watched as he wiped the grime from his hands with a rag. He picked up a remote and muted the iPod, which was docked on a speaker.

"That was Dr. Dre, right?" Sandra asked, inclining her head toward the speaker. "The old guy who sells headphones. He's rapping with the other old guy who does the funny movies and beer commercials."

Stuart laughed. "Old guys to you, but they'll always be N.W.A. to me, and back in the day, they were considered controversial and edgy."

"If you say so." Sandra shrugged at the notion of those old dudes or her conservative father ever being cool.

Stuart opened the minifridge and pulled out a can of orange soda. "Want one?"

She shook her head and silently reviewed her game plan.

Crawl, beg, retract.

She stared at the SS emblem on the grille of the Chevelle. The car was a heap when her father had had it towed home years ago, so covered in rust she hadn't been able to determine its original color.

Now the muscle car was painted in her father's fraternity colors, gold with two wide black stripes down the middle of the hood, and its finish gleamed like Murano glass under the garage lights.

Sandra cleared her throat, and her father looked at her expectantly. "I came over to talk to you about Thanksgiving."

He took a long swig of his soda, then placed the can on his workbench. He crossed his arms over his chest and leaned against the Chevelle. "Can't say I haven't expected this visit," he said. "In fact, I thought you'd have come crawling a few days ago to tell me you put your foot in your mouth and wanted to beg off this preposterous offer to cook dinner."

Crawl.

Beg.

The very words that made up her game plan were irksome coming from her father. Pushing them out of her mind, she replaced them with Vicki's wise words instead: *…whatever you do, don't let your dad provoke you into saying something that will get you into even more of a predicament…*

Sandra took a deep breath. All that was left for her to do now was retract.

"Dad, I—"

Her father cut her off. "What in the world made you issue an invitation like that in the first place? You couldn't even manage instant oatmeal without us having to get a brand-new microwave, and it already came in a bowl," he said incredulously. "All you have to do is add water, stir and microwave. Hell, Mason can do that."

Stuart laughed at his own joke.

Sandra bit down on the inside of her lip, hard. Distracted by a three-way phone call with Vicki and Janelle, she'd inadvertently left the metal spoon in the cardboard container, hit the start button on the microwave and walked away. She hadn't seen or heard the sparks until it was too late.

"That happened when I was in high school, Dad. Do you think you can finally let it go?"

He coughed, his laughing fit apparently irritating his throat.

"As I was about to say, I knew there was no way you could possibly pull off a holiday meal. So I've already called Fred and wrangled an invitation for your mother and myself to have Thanksgiving with them. Did I mention Ivy was cooking?"

Her father had just given her the perfect out, Sandra thought. All she had to do was swallow her pride, nod her head and take it.

So do it!

She sighed. She. Just. Couldn't.

"Well, I suggest you call Mr. King and unwrangle that invite, because you already accepted a previous engagement at *your daughter's* house."

"What?"

"You heard me, Dad. I'm cooking dinner for me, you, Mom and Jordan. Mason, too, if his mother doesn't have him for the holiday."

Sandra had no idea how she'd pull it off, but she would. She had to.

"B-but Ivy's cooking—" Stuart stammered.

Sandra cut him off. "Doesn't matter what she's cooking, because you won't be there. You'll be eating at my house."

Her father's eyes narrowed. His expression hardened to the one he wore when things went awry at Woolcott Industries. "So let me get this straight. You expect me to pass on one of Ivy's gourmet meals, and you know it'll be extra special for the holiday. For what? To end up sharing a greasy bucket of take-out fried chicken at that cramped beach shack of yours?"

Sandra squared her shoulders, determined not to show weakness in the face of his stony expression and, she had to admit, logical argument.

"But isn't Thanksgiving really about being with family?" she asked, answering his question with one of her own.

Eyes identical to hers stared back at her. "Yeah, a family surrounded by a scrumptious feast. Not a cleaning crew or the fire department."

"My dinner will be good, Dad," Sandra said with more confidence that she felt.

She was a competent adult. Surely she could overcome her mishap-ridden past in the kitchen and successfully put one meal on the table.

Her father grunted, picked up his soda and took a big gulp. He put the can on his workbench, and then Sandra caught a nearly imperceptible glint in his eyes.

"You sound pretty sure of yourself," he said. "What if it doesn't turn out good?"

"It will," Sandra insisted.

"Then you wouldn't have a problem making a tiny wager with your old dad?"

Sandra arched a brow. "What kind of wager?"

A grin accompanied the now obvious gleam in her father's eyes. "If your dinner ends up the inedible fiasco I expect it to be, the next time Dale Mills asks you out you'll say yes."

"Dale." Sandra said the name as if Stuart had put a leash on a skunk and asked her to walk it around the block.

"He's a fine young man who's shown quite an interest in you. If you'd just give him a chance, you'd see he's a great guy."

Sandra rolled her eyes skyward. All Dale Mills had an interest in was brownnosing his way up the ladder at Woolcott Industries. Romancing the boss's daughter was just part of it.

Stuart stroked his gray-flecked goatee. "If you can put an edible dinner on the table, like you say, then you've got nothing to lose, right?"

Sandra took in her father leaning against the Chevelle. His grin had morphed into a smug smirk. He'd put her on the spot, and he damn well knew it.

However, she *was* his daughter. "You sound pretty sure of yourself," she said, flipping the script.

"I'm already thinking how pleased Dale will be when you agree to go out with him."

"Then you won't mind upping the ante on your proposed wager?" If she was going to have the possibility of a date with his protégé hanging over her head, then her father would have to put something on the line, too.

Something big.

She eyed the Chevelle.

Stuart followed her gaze and turned his head to look back at the car. When he faced her again, his smug expression was replaced with shock.

"You're kidding, right?" He stood up straight and stared at her, openmouthed.

Sandra folded her arms across her chest, mimicking his earlier action. "Big talk calls for big stakes. So if I manage to pull off a tasty Thanksgiving meal, the Chevelle's mine."

Stuart reached for the can of soda and finished it in one gulp. He stroked his chin again as he thought it over.

"Well?" Sandra prodded.

"If I agree, we're not talking about just any meal. I want to sit down to turkey basted in that sage butter seasoning I like so much, surrounded by all the trimmings—green beans, sweet potatoes and dessert. I'm thinking something with apples. Pie, strudel, I'm not picky." He jabbed his finger in her direction. "However, every morsel must be cooked by *you and you only.*"

Sandra swallowed. So much for her idea of keeping it simple with maybe a chicken or a couple of little Cornish hens.

Stuart shut the hood of the car and smoothed a hand over its shiny finish. "Also, if I'm going to put my girlfriend here on the line, you're going to have to put up bigger stakes."

"Like what?" For goodness' sake, she already had to figure out how in the heck she was going to turn out this meal or go on a date with, *blech*, Dale.

"Five dates with Dale." Her father held up his hand and wiggled his fingers. "And *you'll* ask *him* out."

"M-me?" Sandra stuttered over the single word.

Stuart dusted his palm on his coveralls before extending it to her. "Do we have a bet?"

She stared down at her father's hand for a long moment before finally clasping it. They shook once, sealing their bargain.

"I just hope I'm released from the emergency room, where I'm sure to be getting my stomach pumped Thanksgiving night, in time to see you and my future son-in-law, Dale, head off on your first date. I trust you'll take him someplace nice."

Sandra opened her mouth to respond, but was stopped by the sound of knocking, and they both turned in the direction of the side door.

"Come in," her father yelled.

The door opened and Dale Mills stepped through it, holding a cardboard box. He wore a wool coat over a charcoal suit and slightly askew burgundy tie. An eager grin, akin to that of a dog awaiting a pat on the head from its master, was plastered on his face.

It got even bigger the moment he saw Sandra.

"Dale, what brings you out here, *son*?" Stuart emphasized the last word, an endearment Sandra knew was more for her ears than his employee.

It wasn't that Dale was a bad guy, Sandra thought. In fact, the executive would tick the boxes on most women's husband-material checklist.

However, the over-the-top sucking up grated Sandra's nerves. Even if she had been attracted to him, pleasing her father and Woolcott Industries would always be Dale Mills's number one priority.

Sandra had learned her lesson the hard way. Never again would she fall for a man who couldn't put her first.

Dale held the box out to her father. "It took some doing, but I managed to locate the special brand of car wax you mentioned trying to find. I bought you an entire case of it. I wanted to bring it over before I left for the business meeting in Miami."

He turned to Sandra, but his words were directed at his boss. "If I'd known your lovely daughter would be visiting today, I would have brought flowers."

Give me a break, Sandra thought, and then listened

to make sure she hadn't accidentally uttered the words aloud.

"Nice seeing you, Dale," she said, as both a hello and a goodbye, before he could try asking her out again.

"Dad." Her gaze flicked to the Chevelle. "Don't put too much elbow grease into a wax job, because after I win your girlfriend on Thanksgiving, I'm thinking of painting her pink."

It was nearly midnight when Isaiah got back to his parents' house Thursday night. With the exception of driving his father down to Boston, he'd spent every waking hour of the past three days planning, painting and constructing the Martine's Fine Furnishings' sponsored Halloween fun house.

A large white frame tent had been erected in the parking lot behind the recreation center. It currently boasted a striped effect thanks to the efforts of employee volunteers from Martine's armed with spools of orange reflective tape. The inside had been sectioned off into three areas, one for the caterers to set up the free concessions and stainless-steel washtubs brimming with candy, a middle section for the makeshift fun house's attractions and a third for a few animals coming from a nearby farm.

Isaiah had spent the majority of his time on the attractions, throwing himself into their redesign. As he worked, all afternoon and well into the evening, his thoughts had drifted to spending the next two years at the Royal Academy of Arts in London, immersed in sketching, painting and most of all creating.

But at night his dreams went rogue.

Rolling his stiff shoulders, he stifled a yawn with

his fist. There were still some finishing touches to do, such as transforming the cheap flexible mirrors he'd picked up into reflection-distorting fun house mirrors with a little bending and foam board.

They'd have to wait until tomorrow. He yawned again and hoped his exhaustion would lead to a dreamless, Sandra Woolcott–free sleep. The first since seeing her at The Quarterdeck Monday night.

Isaiah unlocked the back door to find his mother still awake. A plate of cookies had been placed on the kitchen table. She wore a placid maternal smile and the flannel robe covered in pink hearts he'd given her for her birthday when he was ten.

"Good, you're home." She retrieved a carton of milk from the refrigerator.

In any other house, with any other mother, it would be a heartwarming scene reminiscent of a Norman Rockwell portrait. In this house, with his mother, it was a strategic maneuver.

A four-star admiral had nothing on Cecily Martine Jacobs, Isaiah thought.

"I'm not hungry, Mom."

Like a combatant who knew he didn't stand a chance, the best thing for him tonight was a quick retreat. "I'm beat and I smell like paint. I just want to shower and turn in."

His mom poured the milk into glasses as if she hadn't heard him. "You've been occupied with preparations for the Halloween party all week," she said. "Surely you can spare a few minutes for a midnight snack with your mother."

She'd fired her first salvo, and it had been a direct hit.

Guilt—undefeated.

Isaiah sighed. "Of course I can."

He washed his hands at the kitchen sink and took a seat at the table. He plucked a cookie off the plate. Peanut butter, his favorite.

"Thanks for the cookies," he said, popping it into his mouth.

"The rest of the bag is hidden in the laundry room, where your father won't find it," his mother said. "Keeping him on this diet has been challenging, to say the least."

"So are you looking forward to spending Halloween in Salem?" Isaiah asked.

According to his father, she'd also worried that a day of playing tourist would exhaust him, but had finally agreed to go last night.

Cecily nodded. A hint of a smile touched her lips. "He threatened to go without me," she said. "Somebody has to keep an eye on him."

Isaiah washed a second cookie down with a gulp of milk.

"Besides, you're here to keep an eye on things at Martine's now."

Here we go, Isaiah thought. The real reason behind the cozy motherly scene he'd walked into. Not that his mom didn't love him. She did. However, she'd never served him milk and cookies after school as a boy.

Raised to be self-sufficient, he'd always got his own snack. By the time he was twelve, he'd cooked dinner on nights his parents were held up at the office.

"I'm representing our family for *one evening* as a favor to Dad," he said firmly. "Since I'll be there anyway, I thought I'd make a few improvements so it would be more fun for the kids."

His mother looked up from the cookie she was nibbling on. "Word around the office is you've turned it into quite the event. My head of sales was out today, because he'd volunteered to hang ghost piñatas at that tent of yours. Meanwhile, my assistant was more interested in securing a cotton candy machine and a clown costume than working this afternoon," she said. "And did I hear right? Is there actually going to be a petting zoo?"

Isaiah shook his head. "Nothing that elaborate. Just a few animals from a farm in North Andover."

Cecily put the half-eaten cookie back on the plate. She stared across the table at him, rubbing her index finger across her chin.

"Still, I can't help thinking that if you infused Martine's with your youth, ideas and energy, put that economics degree you earned at the naval academy to good—"

"Stop," Isaiah interrupted. He reached out and placed his hand over hers. "You know that's not going to happen. I don't want to work at Martine's. I've never wanted to work at Martine's."

Cecily pulled her hand back. "Do you think I did? Do you really think furniture was my dream career?" she asked, but didn't wait for a response.

She pushed away from the table. Standing, she began to pace the kitchen.

Now this was the mother he knew, Isaiah thought. The only thing missing was the business suit and staccato click of her heels against the hardwood floors.

"I did it. I do it, because I've got Martine blood running through my veins." She stopped and pointed a finger at him. "Just like you."

Returning to her chair, she put her hand over his.

"Don't you see, Isaiah?" Her eyes implored him to understand. "I'm there because it's my duty and my legacy, and now it's yours, too."

A shrewd businesswoman, his mother presented a convincing argument. It might have swayed him, if ten years ago he hadn't allowed the same argument to change the course of his life.

Duty, tradition and *legacy* were the words his father had used when Isaiah had come to him his senior year of high school with an acceptance letter to the prestigious School of the Art Institute of Chicago.

The letter had described the portfolio of his drawings and paintings as outstanding. He'd hoped the enthusiastic response from the world-renowned institution would finally prove to his father that art was more than a hobby for Isaiah.

It was his passion.

He had been devastated when his father shut down the idea. In Ben's mind, his son's future had been decided before he was even born. He wouldn't hear of him doing anything but following in his footsteps through the doors of the U.S. Naval Academy.

"Duty and legacy, son." Cecily repeated the words, breaking into his thoughts. She squeezed his hand.

This time, Isaiah was the one to pull away. He'd let those words control him once, but he wasn't an eighteen-year-old kid anymore. He'd done his duty by being a good sailor. He'd upheld the legacy of both the Martine and Jacobs names by being a good son.

In doing so, he'd given up his own dreams and hurt the girl he used to love more than life itself.

He'd gone from his parents' rules to the navy's rules. Isaiah had earned the right to finally live by his own.

"No," he said, a single word that left no room for misinterpretation, compromise or argument. "I leave for London the day after Thanksgiving. I've been accepted at an art school there, and I'm taking a few weeks to settle in and find studio space to rent before the semester starts in January."

His heart clenched as he watched the hopeful look on his mother's face slide away. Suddenly, she looked tired, and older than her years.

Cecily rose from the table, but paused on her way out of the kitchen. "You've wanted to be an artist ever since you could hold a crayon in your little fist. I thought your father had put an end to it years ago when he ripped up the letter from that big school in Chicago," she said softly.

No man wanted to disappoint his mother, but he wouldn't live his life for her, either.

"It didn't," Isaiah said. "All he did was postpone the inevitable."

Chapter 5

A second consultation with Octavia Hall on Friday had run longer than Sandra expected.

Her client had quickly reviewed the proposed designs and selected one within minutes. She'd also agreed with Sandra's choice of fabric. Unfortunately, she'd spent nearly two hours sounding off on the latest humiliation suffered at the hands of her soon-to-be ex-husband and his much younger girlfriend.

Apparently, the girlfriend was riding around Wintersage in a brand-new Lexus courtesy of Mr. Hall.

Finally home, Sandra quickly donned her Halloween costume and swept her hair into a high ponytail. Her date would be arriving to pick her up soon. It had been a long week, and she was looking forward to a well-deserved night out.

She was tying her hair with a red ribbon when she

heard a familiar ringtone coming from the direction of her purse. Unearthing the phone from her bag, she glanced at her date's number on the screen.

"I'm running a little behind, but I'm almost ready," she said into the cell.

Sandra listened as her date, en route and only a few minutes away from her place, explained he'd been called back into the office by the senior partner at his law firm. The rest of what he had to say faded into background noise.

Blah, blah. Apology. Blah, blah. Rain check.

The result was she was all dressed up and now had no place to go.

Sandra started to toss the phone back into her purse, but changed her mind. Instead, she swiped her fingertips across the small screen. Two rings later, Vicki answered.

"I thought you were going to a Halloween party down in Boston with some lawyer?" her friend asked.

"He had to cancel." Sandra fidgeted with the hem of her short skirt with her free hand. "I don't want to waste a perfectly good costume, and wondered if you wanted to meet up at The Quarterdeck? I'll treat you to one of those pumpkin martinis."

But none for me, she thought, remembering the sweet cocktail had packed quite a wallop. Two drinks had left her hallucinating and conjuring up images of her teenage boyfriend, all grown up and looking good enough to eat.

She heard her friend's weary sigh on the other end of the phone. Vicki had also put in extralong hours all week playing catch-up at work.

"I'm beat," she said. "In fact, I'm already in my pajamas nursing a glass of white wine."

Sandra pulled the phone away from her ear just long enough to double-check the time. "In your pj's at seven o'clock on a Friday night?"

"Exactly. Now I'm trying to figure out a way to put an end to my spending Friday and Saturday nights alone."

"Slipping into a smoking-hot outfit and coming out with me would be a start." Sandra heard the sound of paper rustling in the background.

"That's part of my problem. I don't own any hot outfits. Never mind the fact that I'd just be sitting around watching men ogle you."

"Vicki Ahlfors, you know good and well I'd never abandon you to run off with some guy."

"Not intentionally," her friend said. "But with Janelle married and you usually out on a date most weekend nights, I either have to figure out what to do with myself, or buy a cat for company like other lonely single women."

Sandra plopped down on her sofa, knowing there was little chance of her convincing her to join her tonight. "Oh, come on. You're gorgeous. It's just a matter of time before your Mr. Right comes along."

She could almost see Vicki shrugging.

"If he did, he'd probably walk right past me."

Sandra heard the rustling sound again. "I'm not following you."

"What I'm trying to say is it's about time I stopped hoping and waiting for the perfect man, and did something about attracting him," Vicki said. "I stopped by the newsstand on the way home and picked up a stack of hairstyle and fashion magazines."

Sandra sat upright, her mouth hanging open in surprise. "You're thinking about getting rid of your *Little House on the Prairie* schoolmarm bun?" she asked, unable to imagine her friend without her long hair pulled back in the style she'd worn for years.

"It's not a bun. It's a chignon," Vicki argued. "And—"

"It's both functional and elegant," Sandra interrupted. She'd heard Vicki say the words enough times to know them by heart. "Anyway, if you need any help in the fashion department, we can schedule a big shopping trip when Janelle returns from her honeymoon."

"Whatever I decide to do, I need to do it on my own. So it reflects my personal style, not yours or Janelle's."

Sandra opened her mouth to say she understood, when the doorbell rang. "Somebody's at my door," she said instead.

"Maybe your date can make it, after all."

"It's probably just some trick-or-treaters."

"Doubt it. Every kid in town is over at the rec center party."

Sandra agreed, and her hopes lifted at the possibility that Vicki was right, and she might not have to sit at home alone dressed in full Halloween regalia, after all.

The doorbell rang again, followed by a pounding on the door.

"Well, I'm going back to my magazines. Talk to you later," Vicki said, ending the call.

Sandra peered through the peephole and smiled when she saw a little body all decked out in a miniature Patriots uniform. She unlocked the door and threw it wide-open. An ocean breeze, unseasonably warm for the end of October, ushered her nephew and brother inside.

"Hey, you!" She immediately lifted the baby from Jordan's arms and covered his chubby cheeks in kisses. "How's my little Super Bowl champ doing tonight?"

Mason rewarded her with giggles and drool.

Sandra looked over her nephew's head at his father. Weariness had etched fine lines in the dark circles under Jordan's eyes, and he looked as if he hadn't had a decent night's sleep in ages. Taking in her outfit, her brother closed his red-rimmed eyes briefly and pinched the bridge of his nose before gazing at her again.

"Of course, you already have plans this evening. It's Friday night." He seemed to be talking more to himself than to her.

"Good to see you, too."

"Sorry, it's just that Allison was a no-show," he muttered, pacing the small entryway. "And Mom and Dad have plans."

"Jordan."

He ran a hand over his short-cropped hair. "I was supposed to be at the Windom campaign headquarters hours ago. All the polls show him running ahead of Darren Howerton, but this is the last weekend before the election, on Tuesday. We need to give it one last push. There's so much to do."

"Jordan." Sandra tried again.

"I tried working from home, but Mason woke up from his nap and started getting into everything."

"Jordan," Sandra repeated louder.

Her nephew made a squawking sound in an attempt to mimic her that finally got her brother's attention.

She reached out and touched Jordan's arm. "I'll babysit."

"But you're obviously dressed for a Halloween party."

Sandra adjusted her nephew on her hip. "You're getting heavy," she told the toddler, then turned to her brother. "My date canceled at the last minute, so I'm free tonight."

Jordan heaved a sigh, and she could almost see the pressure lift from his shoulders. "Are you sure?" he asked, already draping Mason's diaper bag over her free arm. "I owe you one."

She smiled. "Um…Jordan, seeing as how this favor officially puts you in my debt, I was thinking you…"

Her brother was already shaking his head. "No way," he said. "Anything but that."

"But—" Sandra began.

"Dad already told me all about the big Thanksgiving wager, and I don't want any part of your trial run experiments. Neither does my son."

"No!" Mason declared.

Jordon rubbed his son's head. "Smart boy."

"Come on, if I win the Chevelle, I promise to let you borrow it," she bargained.

Her brother appeared to think it over. In all these years, no one had ever been allowed behind the wheel of the classic muscle car but their father.

Finally, Jordan shook his head. "Not worth the risk to my stomach."

"But I'm doing you a favor tonight," Sandra argued.

"And I'm paying you back with a little advice," her brother said. "You have a lot of great qualities, but cooking isn't one of them. You can't win. Back out of this bet."

"I can't do that," Sandra said.

"Then I suggest you start thinking about where you're going to take ass-kissing Dale on those dates." Jordan turned to walk to his car.

"That's not going to happen," she called out to his retreating back.

She could hear his laughter over the sounds of the nearby ocean waves as she shut the door.

"You believe in your auntie, don't you, baby?" Sandra shifted her nephew on her hip.

Mason bobbed his head as if he actually understood.

She looked at the both of them dressed in their costumes, and an idea popped into her head. "How would you like Auntie to take you to your first Halloween party?"

Mason chortled. Again, he bobbed his head as if he'd understood her. "Bye!"

She pressed a kiss against his cheek. "Let's go party!"

Chapter 6

The sound of children laughing, the smell of popcorn and the occasional bleating of a goat filled the tent Isaiah had set up behind the recreation center. For one night only, it was the official home of Wintersage's Halloween carnival fun house.

Isaiah had been so busy pulling the whole thing together that the party was in full swing before he had a moment to check out the results of his efforts. He stood in the middle of the large area between the food concessions and the mini petting zoo, and panned the inside of the tent.

Pint-size princesses, superheroes and everything in between lined up to play the games he'd breathed new life into with fresh paint and updated designs. The kids' excited expressions, combined with the feeling of having created something, filled him with a deep satisfaction military life never had.

An elbow jabbed his side. Tony, dressed up in a ring-master's costume, handed him a paper cup filled with fruit punch.

"I can hardly believe these games are the same heap of trash I saw a few days ago," he said. "Just so you know, my oldest gave the clown dartboard a thumbs-up, and that's a high compliment with the eight-year-old crowd."

Isaiah raised his paper cup to his friend and drank the punch in one gulp. He glanced at the ancient dartboard he'd revamped with a lazy Susan, paint and foam board. "Glad they're enjoying it."

"Man, the kids are all having a blast. You should have seen this party last year and the year before. The children were high on sugar and bored out of their minds." Tony slapped him on the back. "You did good."

Isaiah looked over his old teammate's shoulder. "So which of these kids are your three monsters?"

Laughing, Tony started to scan the tent in search of his offspring.

"Damn!"

"What's wrong?" Isaiah looked around the game area, relieved there didn't appear to be any accidents.

"Um… If I show you something, do you promise not to go running into a post and cracking your head open again?"

"Huh?" Isaiah frowned. He had no idea where his friend was going with this one.

Tony nodded toward the concessions. Isaiah turned and saw a vision straight out of his dreams the night before.

Sandra Woolcott all dressed up like a cheerleader.

It couldn't be. Isaiah blinked. Hard. To make sure it wasn't his imagination.

While his brain worked to separate last night's fantasy from tonight's reality, his greedy gaze moved on its own accord. It ate up the sight of her standing in line at the cotton candy machine.

But not even spun sugar could compete with his sweet view of legs that would make a Rockette weep with envy.

Isaiah started at her ankles and inched upward, slowly caressing the smooth dark skin of her shapely calves with his eyes. He lingered there a moment to catch his breath and send a silent shout out to the costume's short skirt for providing a delectable real-life view of toned thighs he'd imagined spread open to him the night before.

Tony hadn't exaggerated his description of the all-grown-up Sandra, Isaiah thought. Knockout curves in all the right places.

Then his gaze lit upon the one thing, or rather *person*, his old teammate hadn't thought to mention.

A baby.

Nor had Isaiah asked.

He looked at the toddler in her arms pointing at the cotton candy machine, and watched as she kissed the top of the kid's head.

Deep down, Isaiah hadn't wanted to know whether she was married, with a family of her own. Especially after he'd seen her the other night at The Quarterdeck, looking so unbelievably beautiful.

He felt an elbow at his side.

"You okay?" Tony asked.

Isaiah nodded, still staring at Sandra and the little

boy. He speculated that she probably had more kids than this one. And with them came a man, who had been smart enough to make her his wife.

The rigid posture drummed into Isaiah at Annapolis slumped a notch, along with his mood. The sight before him made it official. Sandra Woolcott would belong to him only in the past or in his dreams.

"Yeah, I'm good," he told his friend.

"Are you sure? Because you look like you did the day you ran headfirst into that goalpost."

Isaiah felt as if he'd taken a hit, but shook it off, along with proprietary feelings over a girl that up until now he'd only ever thought of as his. Exhaling, he squared his shoulders. "I'm headed over to say hello."

Tony muttered something about finding his wife and kids, but his voice faded into the background as Isaiah made his way to the concession area. A few people stopped him along the way to either welcome him home or rave about how their children were enjoying this year's party. He responded on cue with automatic polite responses, but his gaze remained trained on the cheerleader buying cotton candy for the delighted little football player in her arms.

"You can't stuff the whole thing in your mouth," Sandra said as the toddler reached for the pink ball of fluff with both hands. She appeared to have her own hands full balancing the boy, an oversize blue bag and the cone of spun sugar. "Give me a moment, baby, and I'll break you off a piece."

Her back was to him, but Isaiah could hear the amusement in her tone as she pulled the cotton candy out of the kid's reach with her free arm.

"Mine!" The boy shouted and pointed at it. When he

didn't get immediate satisfaction, he suddenly lunged for it. The quick move threw Sandra off balance and she stumbled backward.

Instinctively, Isaiah stepped forward, catching mother, son and candy floss in one swoop.

"I got you," he said, trying not to think about how good she felt in his arms. He felt her steady herself, and slowly released his hold.

Only his fingertips remained on her arms.

"Thank you," she said, finally turning around. "That was a close call…"

"No problem," Isaiah said.

Sandra stared up at him, openmouthed. With her hair in a ponytail and the wide-eyed gaze, she looked like the teenage girl he'd once loved with everything in him.

"Isaiah," she whispered.

A beginning of a smile graced her full lips. It zapped Isaiah back ten years, and for an instant, she was still the girl who waited for him after football games. The girl he'd taken for a ride in his truck the day he'd received his driver's license. The girl he'd taught to sketch in art class.

His very best friend.

As Sandra recovered from the surprise of seeing him, he watched her expression transform. Guileless turned guarded, erecting an invisible shield between them that had never before existed.

"How long have you been back?" Her tone was detached.

It was just as well, Isaiah decided. The familiarity of the woman was just an illusion. A decade had come and gone. She was somebody's mother now, and more than likely someone's wife.

"A week." His own words came out stiff and awkward.

In his head, they were having an entirely different conversation. One where he eschewed pride and propriety and simply spoke his truth.

I've missed you.

Sandra broke off a piece of cotton candy for the baby, who grabbed her hand and shoved the pink fluff into his open mouth. "Are you on leave visiting your folks?"

"Visiting, but not on leave. I've completed my military stint."

Even as he spoke, his internal monologue continued.

I saw you at The Quarterdeck Monday evening and have dreamed of you every night since.

"So you're not planning to settle in Wintersage?"

He shook his head.

Even if I had been, there's no way I could now. Seeing you with your husband and children would be too difficult.

"Well, you look great," she said.

Her tongue slid over her pouty bottom lip in a gesture he knew was unconscious, which somehow made it sexier.

"So do you."

I've seen women from all over the world. Not one as stunning as you.

The baby made a squawking noise and pointed at the cotton candy torch. Sandra smiled at the boy, a genuine grin that made Isaiah envious of a toddler.

It was hell getting over you ten years ago.

She broke off another piece and fed it to her son.

"Good?" she asked.

The kid nodded. He gobbled up the treat quickly and then pointed a sticky finger at Isaiah.

"How rude of me. I forgot to introduce you," Sandra crooned to the boy as she readjusted him on her hip. "Mason, this is Isaiah, and Isaiah, meet my nephew, Mason."

"Nephew?" Isaiah asked.

She nodded. "He's Jordan's little boy."

His gaze dropped to her left hand. No ring.

Yes!

He couldn't explain it. Nor did it make a lick of sense. But the revelation made him feel like a doomed man who'd just received a last-minute reprieve from the guillotine.

"You thought he was mine." The words were more of a statement than a question. Her gaze trailed his to her ringless finger, and then rose to his face.

There was a time when Sandra could tell with one look exactly what was on his mind. As they stood there staring at each other, Isaiah wondered if she still could. He wondered if she knew just how badly he wanted her right now.

Her brown eyes widened as realization dawned. An almost smile tugged at the corners of her mouth, and for an instant it was if they'd never spent more than a day apart.

"You're not serious," she said.

As she shook her head, he nodded his.

This time he said what he meant, no longer having to hold back because he thought she was another man's wife.

"Oh, I'm *very* serious."

A spark filled with wicked promise flashed in her eyes, but vanished so quickly he thought he was mistaken. She continued to stare at him as she broke off another piece of cotton candy and gave it to her nephew.

"Tell Mr. Jacobs goodbye, so we can go see the bunnies."

"Bye!" The kid shouted over a mouthful of pink fluff.

Isaiah watched his favorite cheerleader walk across the tent to the petting zoo. He couldn't take his eyes off her. As he stood mesmerized by the generous curve of her ass swaying beneath the short skirt, he wondered how he could have ever thought he was over her?

Sandra didn't have to turn around to know Isaiah was staring at her.

She felt it.

Hotter than the warmth radiating off his body when he'd caught her in his arms, the searing heat of his dark-eyed gaze blazed a trail up her bare legs. Her skin tingled in the wake of his eyes skimming the backs of her calves and thighs. She felt them, as if they were his hands lingering on her backside as she continued to walk away.

So much had changed over the years, Sandra thought, but two things remained the same.

For one, she could still tell with a look what Isaiah was thinking. Secondly, time hadn't extinguished the chemistry between them, ignited the day they'd met in art class. It had merely put it on a slow simmer.

And tonight it had nearly boiled over.

Thank goodness she had Mason in tow. Her babysitting duties had been the only thing stopping her from doing something impetuous like inviting Isaiah Jacobs back to her place *and her bed*.

To finally have what they'd denied themselves as teenagers. Although they'd come close.

"Dog!" Mason's delighted squeal corralled her wayward thoughts. He pointed to a baby goat as they approached the area with the animals. "Dog!"

Sandra snapped back into auntie mode. "That's not a dog. It's a goat. Can you say goat?"

"Dog! Dog! Dog!"

She laughed and tossed the paper cone from the cotton candy into a trash can, then set the toddler on his feet. He raised his arms over his head and made a beeline to the edge of the small pen, pressing his belly against the fence.

"Dog!" He reached his chubby hands out toward the baby goats.

A middle-aged woman wearing jeans and a T-shirt bearing the name of a farm came over to them. She crouched down on her haunches. "Hello, there." She addressed Mason first and then looked up at Sandra. "He's welcome to come inside the pen."

Sandra thought about how rough her nephew could be, and feared one of the animals taking a nip out of him if he inadvertently pulled or tugged at them too hard.

The woman must have detected her hesitance. "They're all extremely gentle and love the contact nearly as much as the youngsters do."

Sandra saw other children milling around the enclosure, some as young as Mason, playing with the menagerie of ducks, bunnies, sheep, chickens and goats. Finally, she lifted him over the short fence into the makeshift pen and stepped in behind him.

Mason quickly made friends with a small black-and-white goat, which had no problems being addressed as a dog. As Sandra laughed at her nephew's antics, she couldn't help regretting that her brother was missing these funny moments.

Maybe Jordan didn't have to miss out, she thought.

Reaching into her bag, Sandra pulled out her cell phone. She switched on its video camera and began recording her nephew as he hugged a brown goat and then rested his head on its back.

"Wave at the camera, Mason," she coaxed.

"Bye!" He grinned, moving his little hand through the air.

The woman with the farm T-shirt returned, a loaf of bread in her hand and a smiling toddler clinging to each leg of her jeans. "We're headed over to feed the ducks." She inclined her head toward the fowl on the other side of the small pen. "Would your little one like to help?"

Sandra nodded her permission. Mason took the worker's extended hand, and they walked a few feet away to the ducks, a brown baby goat trailing behind them.

Sandra snapped a few shots of her nephew with the animals. As she texted them to her brother, she felt a warm tingle at the back of her neck.

Her hand went to the skin there, where gooseflesh had started to form. Sandra spun around to see what, deep down, she already knew.

Isaiah.

Their gazes connected across the tent, and she licked her suddenly dry lips. He was indeed watching her.

And he looked damn hot doing it.

The mayor sidled up to him, and Isaiah turned to talk to him, breaking the connection.

Still, Sandra ogled him openly. The boy she'd known

had been tall and lanky, all knees and elbows. The man she was practically leering at now was an altogether different story.

Wide shoulders and a broad chest tested the limits of a black polo shirt, whose short sleeves revealed muscular biceps. She'd felt their strength when his arms had wrapped around her after she'd stumbled, and she couldn't help imagining what it would feel like to be wrapped in them all night.

Her gaze slipped lower, to his jeans. Sandra wondered whether he could feel the heat of her stare on that nice ass of his, just as she'd felt his earlier.

Isaiah turned away from the mayor and gazed directly at her. She averted her eyes, but not before she saw the look of raw desire in his.

Down, girl! Sandra issued herself a silent warning.

She'd seen the man, what? Just twenty minutes ago? And already she was acting as if he had a roll of cookie dough shoved down the front of his jeans.

Shaking her head at her own ridiculousness, she looked down at her nephew, who was happily babbling at the ducks. Isaiah was in her past, and that's exactly where any connection she had with him, real or imagined, belonged.

She looked over her shoulder for what she told herself was one last peek at him.

What would it hurt to have him just one time? her inner bad girl thought, rising up. *One no-strings, sexy time*.

He was grown. She was grown. Why not? Sandra started to buy into the idea. It wasn't as if he was even staying in Wintersage.

Then her common sense showed up. The killjoy immediately shut down the notion of steamy sex with Isaiah Jacobs.

Get your nephew, it warned. *And take your hot tail home.*

Chapter 7

What in the hell are you doing?

Isaiah braced his hands against either side of the doorjamb and lowered his head until it touched Sandra's front door.

He'd spent hours trying to talk himself out of coming here, staying at the rec center long after the party had ended. He'd even tried wearing himself out by helping dismantle the tent and restoring the area behind the building to a parking lot.

It hadn't worked.

"Go home," he whispered. She'd never have to know he had come here.

But his body refused the direct order. It stood steadfast, not caring that he had no reasonable explanation for being there, or the very real possibility of Sandra slamming the door in his face.

All Isaiah knew was he had to see her again.

Now.

Exhaling, he slid one hand down to the doorbell and pressed. The chime preceded one of the longest minutes of his life.

"Forget something?" he heard her ask through the door, before it swung open.

Sandra held out the blue diaper bag he'd seen slung over her shoulder earlier. He watched her brown eyes widen at the sight of him.

Before either of them had time to think, Isaiah wrapped an arm around her waist and pulled her to him. She gasped as she stared up at him, and he caught the scent of cotton candy on her breath.

"Yeah, I forgot this."

He leaned in and captured those pouty lips of hers—lips that had played a starring role in his dreams for four nights straight—in a kiss.

Her mouth was everything he'd anticipated and more, pillow soft and tinged with spun sugar.

Sandra's hands rose to his chest, and her fingers splayed against his pecs. Isaiah braced himself for her rejection, expecting to be shoved away any minute and his kiss rebuffed.

Instead, she fisted the collar of his jacket and tugged him closer as she parted her lips.

The silent invitation combined with the soft, sweet taste of her mouth unleashed the pent-up desire he'd carried around for days, thinking about all the things he wanted to do to her, with her.

A groan sounded low in his throat as she pressed those luscious curves against him. Her heat enveloped him. It penetrated his clothes as if the two of them were skin on skin.

Isaiah hardened instantly.

His cock nudged her belly, but his tongue continued to leisurely stroke hers. Tasting, reacquainting itself with every nuance of her sexy mouth. They kissed as if the other were the cure to an illness they didn't know they'd had.

When they finally came up for air, he was the first one to speak. Although the last thing he wanted to do right now was talk.

Once upon a time, he'd loved this woman as much as a teenage boy could. While he no longer loved her, he'd always care deeply for her. Enough to be crystal clear, before tonight went any further.

He leaned down until his forehead touched hers. "I haven't been able to get you out of my head since I saw you at The Quarterdeck Monday night."

"So that *was* you." She lifted her head, their eyes meeting.

Isaiah nodded. "I'd thought I was over you. But I think of you. I dream of you…" His voice trailed off.

He cleared his throat and began to speak from his head, not his crotch. "But for the first time in my adult life, I'm not government property. I fulfilled my duty and obligation to both my folks and Uncle Sam."

Isaiah knew what he had to say would probably shut down any chance of tonight going beyond their kiss, but it had to be said. "So while I want you, badly, more than I've ever wanted any other woman, I'm not looking for a relationship with you, with anyone."

Sandra's face remained impassive as she stared up at

him. Isaiah still held her flush against him. Her hands still gripped the collar of his jacket.

And he was still hard as a rock.

"I shouldn't have come here," he said finally.

"I should send you away," she said.

"But you haven't."

"Not yet."

"Why?"

She released her grip on his collar. "Because I haven't told you what I want. But first, it's my turn to explain."

Isaiah continued to relish the feel of her body against his, expecting the pleasure to be snatched away at any moment.

Sandra's finger slid down to the center of his chest. "Work is my man, and until I take my design business beyond Wintersage, I won't cheat or shortchange it by diverting my attention with a relationship. Not with you, not with anyone."

As she spoke, Isaiah saw beyond her beauty. He saw ambition, determination and strength. It stirred up an entirely different feeling than the love he'd felt for the young Sandra or the overwhelming lust he had for the grown woman.

Respect.

And it made him want her even more.

"The bottom line is you and I have unfinished business." She tapped her index finger against his chest. "And I have no expectations beyond getting you naked and inside me."

Just when Isaiah thought he couldn't get any harder, he did.

Sandra returned both hands to his chest and pushed

him away. She turned her back to him and walked through her front door.

Automatically, Isaiah's gaze dropped to her bare legs in that short cheerleader skirt, and he mentally calculated how quickly he could have them wrapped around his waist. She was right. Their unfinished business had been deferred long enough.

It was time he took care of it.

She looked back at him over her shoulder. "So are you coming in, or am I going to have to call my vibrator Isaiah all night long?"

He followed her across the threshold, his cock leading the way. He kicked the door closed behind him with his heel as the hypnotic swish of her short skirt beckoned him farther inside.

Visions of the Sandra from his dreams collided with the real-life fantasy and instinct took over.

In one swift movement, Isaiah lifted her up and pinned her to the closest wall. Her arms encircled his shoulders, while he kissed her the way he intended to stroke her—long, hard and endlessly deep.

She ground against him and their bodies moved in time with their mouths. Then, like an answer to his secret prayers, she wrapped those thick thighs around his waist.

"God, yes," Isaiah rasped, wresting his mouth from hers.

He buried his face against her neck and struggled for control. Enveloped in her intoxicating scent, cotton candy mixed with an exotic bottled fragrance, he ran his tongue over the throbbing pulse point at her throat for just a tiny taste.

Sandra gripped his head in her palms and pulled it back.

"Bedroom?" Her question tumbled out of her mouth in a breathless pant. Her legs released their hold on his waist.

"Not yet."

Despite the raging impatience of a certain part of his anatomy, Isaiah refused to rush. It had taken them too long to get here. He intended to draw this moment out all night, touching, kissing, tasting and loving every inch of her until they both were too exhausted to move.

He slid his hands beneath her skirt until they reached the top of her barely there panties. Hooking the waistband with his fingertips, he dropped to one knee as he pulled the scrap of lace over her hips and down her legs.

The sound of her gasp broke the heated silence.

Sandra moved to step out of them, but he stopped her with a shake of his head.

"I've got this." He lifted her sneaker-clad foot off the floor and draped her leg over his shoulder. The move raised the hem of her skirt, exposing her goodies in full view.

Goodies just begging to be tasted.

Isaiah licked his lips. Then he licked her.

"Oh, yes!" Sandra's muffled cry filled his ears, which were snugly cradled between her thighs.

She clasped his head in her hands and rocked against his mouth as his tongue worked her clit with long, languid strokes.

Over and over again. As if pleasing her were his full-time job.

Her back began to slide down the wall, and Isaiah

gripped her hips to steady her. But his tongue remained on task.

Licking.

Flicking.

Sucking.

Until she shook with the tremors of her first orgasm of the night.

Isaiah smiled to himself as he kissed her spot, knowing it certainly wouldn't be her last.

Sandra sagged against the wall. Only Isaiah's firm grip on her hips kept her from dissolving into a puddle of goo on the hardwood floor of her entryway.

She sighed contentedly as he gently lifted her wobbly leg from his shoulder and returned her foot to the floor.

He stood and brushed his lips against hers in the softest of kisses. His breath was warm on her face, and she could taste herself on his mouth.

Their gazes connected and a smile played at Isaiah's lips. "Yum." He uttered the single word in a low whisper that sent aftershocks straight to her core. The full length of his erection pressed against her belly, pinning her back to the wall. Long, thick and hard enough to jackhammer through concrete.

The delicious feel of him turned the satisfaction he'd delivered with his tongue into a distant memory. All she could think about now was the dull ache between her thighs and him filling it.

ASAP.

Sandra pushed him away, but only far enough for her to undo the top button on his jeans. Her teeth sank into her bottom lip as she struggled to lower the zipper over the thick bulge.

Isaiah hissed an expletive through his teeth, before gently pushing her fumbling fingers aside.

"If your hand brushes against me one more time, this is going to be over before it even starts," he said.

He undid the zipper, and Sandra wasted no time shoving his jeans and underwear down to his knees.

Yum. His own word echoed through her head as she stared down at his hard cock. Tearing her eyes away, she met his gaze, and just like when they were teenagers, she knew exactly what he was thinking.

She shook her head from side to side, nixing his thought of continuing this in her bedroom. The minute it would take to get there was sixty seconds too long.

"Right here," she demanded. "Right now."

Sandra pulled herself from the wall. Crossing her arms, she reached for the hem of her top and dragged it up and over her head. Her nipples beaded inside the minuscule cups of her demi-bra at Isaiah's appreciative glance. Not to mention his impressive below-the-waist salute.

A lazy half smile, which she found incredibly sexy, crossed his face. He quickly shed his pants, retrieving a condom from his wallet and then tossing the wallet aside.

He placed the foil packet in her palm. "Hold on to this for me." His eyes dropped to the red lace barely covering her breasts. "I've got other matters to attend to."

Leaning in, Isaiah pressed a kiss to the V between her breasts, before undoing the front clasp of her bra with his teeth.

"God, you're beautiful," he said once her breasts were fully exposed. "Every damn inch of you."

He started in on one breast, and then went to the

other, paying each the same rapt attention he'd given her clit.

Licking.

Flicking.

Sucking.

Sandra moaned his name as she writhed against his cock. Each caress of his hands and tongue made her heart pound and elicited cries of pleasure in rough guttural utterances she barely recognized as her own.

Pinned between the wall and his hard body, she reveled in the erotic confinement, her senses overwhelmed by his touch, his groans, his scent. Everything Isaiah.

Never had Sandra craved a man as much as she desired this one, and she doubted she ever would again.

"Isaiah, please," she begged, when it all became too much and at the same time not enough.

Isaiah covered her mouth with his, dragging her tongue into a slow, deep kiss. Meanwhile, his hands responded to her desperate plea. He lifted her skirt, parting her thighs with his fingers before inserting one inside her.

Sandra gasped at the intimate invasion. The foil edges of the condom packet dug into her palm as she fisted it in her hand.

"You feel so good," Isaiah rasped against her ear, propelling her pulse into a wild, erratic rhythm. "So hot and tight." His shadow of beard scraped against her cheek as he faced her, while his index finger continued to slide in and out of her wetness. "I've ached to touch you like this for so long and already it's exceeded any fantasy."

Their gazes connected, and Sandra stroked her hand down the side of his face.

"You've always been my fantasy," she admitted, staring into his intense dark eyes.

"I think we've both wasted enough time on fantasies." Isaiah withdrew his finger, and Sandra licked her lips in anticipation.

Though they'd lived separate lives for the past decade, it felt as if they'd waited a lifetime for this moment.

Isaiah took the packet from her hand, ripped it open with his teeth and quickly rolled the condom on. He clasped her wrists in one large hand and raised her arms over her head.

"Wrap your legs around my waist."

Supported by the wall behind her, Sandra did as he bade. She gasped as she slowly lowered herself down on him inch by delectable inch.

God, he felt good. So incredibly good.

"Wait." Sandra froze and closed her eyes, savoring the sensation of finally having him inside her.

"You okay?" Isaiah asked.

She opened her eyes and stared into his. "I just needed a second to catch my breath, before I take the ride of my life."

Chapter 8

Isaiah awoke before dawn the next morning with every intention of quietly slipping out of Sandra's bed, finding his clothes and going home.

They'd made their feelings clear last night. Neither of them were interested in a relationship or anything beyond sex.

Damn good sex, he thought. Images from just hours ago played through his mind.

Which probably accounted for him standing in her pitifully stocked kitchen with two grocery bags after a quick trip to the store. Sandra's kitchen, like the rest of her small house, was decorated in a bold, graphic, black-and-white scheme accented with unexpected jolts of color, mostly red or vivid yellow.

Isaiah had been too preoccupied with the woman to notice their surroundings last night, but in the light of day he found himself admiring her tastes. Her home managed to give off both a bright and at the same time serene vibe.

He liked it.

Isaiah opened one of the white cupboard doors and replaced the expired granola bars he'd found there earlier with a fresh box. The stale ones had been the only edible thing on the nearly barren shelves, which contained only mugs and coffee.

Her refrigerator had been empty, too, with the exception of a few bottles of water.

Cooking breakfast was the least he could do after the way he'd shown up on her doorstep last night, Isaiah reasoned. He was hungry anyway, so it wasn't a big deal. He started the coffeemaker while bacon sizzled in the skillet he'd picked up at the store. When he heard Sandra stirring in the bedroom, he added a few eggs.

"Did I die and wake up in heaven?"

Isaiah turned away from the stove to see her standing in front of the breakfast bar. His breath caught at the sight of her wrapped in a red silk robe, and he had to remind himself to exhale. Her pretty face was scrubbed free of makeup. The silky hair he'd tangled his fingers in as they'd made love throughout the night was pulled up in a haphazard ponytail.

"Are you referring to me or the bacon and coffee?" he asked.

Sandra smiled. Now Isaiah knew why he'd returned to her house with groceries. One look from her and he suddenly felt the warmth of her delicious curves pressed against him last night. Her touch. Her taste.

Sandra's voice corralled his wayward thoughts before he gave in to the urge to throw her over his shoulder and take her back to the bed she'd just left.

"Food and a good-looking man cooking are unheard of in my kitchen," she said.

"Obviously." Isaiah used the new spatula to scoop bacon and eggs onto two waiting plates. "How do you manage to feed yourself?"

Sandra seated herself at the breakfast bar. "I don't. Most of my meals are on the go." She looked down at the plate he put in front of her, and her eyes brightened. "I'd forgotten you know how to cook."

In high school, they'd often done their homework or worked on a project for art class at each other's houses. When they'd gone to Sandra's house, the Woolcotts' cook and housekeeper, Milly, had whipped up an after-school snack. At his house, he'd prepared them something quick to eat.

"I just remembered you don't." A chuckle escaped Isaiah's lips as he poured coffee into yellow mugs and slid one across the black granite countertop to her. Memories of the Woolcotts' kitchen after the microwaved oatmeal incident came back to him.

Sandra rolled her eyes and scrunched up her face. "Don't remind me. My pride and my noncooking skills have me in enough trouble right now."

"Trouble?" Isaiah asked from across the breakfast bar.

"Long story." She picked a slice of bacon from her plate and took a bite. She closed her eyes briefly and sighed. "God, I really am in heaven. This is delicious." She polished off the piece of bacon and immediately reached for a second.

"It's the least I could do for my favorite cheerleader," he said, before helping himself to a forkful of eggs.

Sandra averted her eyes as a small, incredibly endearing smile graced her lips. The expression reminded him of the teenage girl he once knew as well as he knew himself.

"So want to tell me about it?" he asked.

The woman on the other side of the breakfast bar was all about her plate. She swallowed the shovelful of eggs she'd stuffed into her mouth, and chased it with more bacon. Isaiah doubted she even heard his question.

"Excuse my manners. It's just that I can't remember the last time I had a real breakfast," Sandra said, between mouthfuls. Finally, she looked up at him. "Did you just ask me something?"

Isaiah moved his bacon from his plate to hers. "You mentioned being in trouble a few minutes ago. Need to talk about it?"

Sandra exhaled. Her shoulders slumped a notch, the subtle movement stirring up unwarranted protective instincts inside him.

"Like I said, it's a long story. I don't want to bother you with it." She waved her hand in a dismissive gesture.

Isaiah knew he should leave it alone. It was none of his business. Yet sitting down and having a conversation with her after so many years took him back to the days when they could tell each other anything.

He reached across the granite counter and covered her hand with his own. "You want to know the real reason I came here last night?" he asked.

She arched a brow. "I'm pretty sure I already do."

Isaiah chuckled. "Maybe that was part of it, and it turned out to be a wonderful reason. However, it wasn't my sole purpose."

He gave her fingers a squeeze, and she looked down

at their joined hands. "You and I once shared a special closeness that went beyond a teenage romance. We were true friends," Isaiah said. "The main reason I came here last night was because I've missed you, Sandra. I've missed my best friend."

She studied his face. "We really were best friends, weren't we?"

Her question was more of a statement. Still, Isaiah nodded his head as she continued.

"Having Janelle and Vicki still in my life made me forget you were more than just a boyfriend to me," she said. "I could always go to them with whatever was on my mind, but it was *you* I told the most important stuff. Things I carried deep down inside."

And he'd hurt her, Isaiah thought. Ancient history neither of them had brought up. Not yet.

He pulled her hand to his lips and pressed a kiss to her open palm. He'd felt the same as she had. He'd never shared the hopes and dreams he'd revealed to her with Tony or the guys he'd hung out with in high school, or even the friends he'd made at Annapolis.

"I'm only in Wintersage until the day after Thanksgiving, but until then I'd really like to have my best friend back," he said. "For just a little while."

Isaiah waited as Sandra appeared to mull over what he'd said. Her answer shouldn't mean this much to him, but for some reason it did.

"I'd like that," she said finally. "I'd like it a lot."

Isaiah busied himself with the breakfast cleanup so she wouldn't see just how happy it made him to have her friendship again. Even if it was only for the next few weeks.

"Anyway, if you need someone to talk to about those

troubles you mentioned earlier, I'm as good a listener now as I was back then," he said, as he topped off both of their coffee mugs.

Sandra shrugged. "It's a long, silly story, but the upshot is I made a bet with my father I could pull off cooking Thanksgiving dinner."

Isaiah struggled to keep his expression neutral. "Could you repeat that?"

"You heard right," Sandra confirmed.

He took a long sip from his mug. "Unless you've somehow learned to cook over the past decade, and by the looks of your kitchen I'm guessing you haven't, *why?*"

Sandra blew out a sigh before spilling the entire story. With coffee mug in hand, Isaiah leaned against the counter and listened. So she'd become a designer, after all, he noted when she got to the part about old man Woolcott dismissing her sketches. Isaiah resisted the urge to interrupt and instead made a mental note to ask more about Swoon Couture later.

After all, they had the next month to catch up, he reminded himself.

"Wow, you do have a situation on your hands," he said, when she was done. "What's your plan?"

Sandra climbed off the stool and padded barefoot from the kitchen. She returned moments later carrying a load of cookbooks in her arms.

"I checked these out of the library yesterday." She dumped them on the breakfast bar and sat down again.

Isaiah picked up a few of the books and quickly thumbed through them. They were authored by top chefs made famous through television food channels, and the covers featured picture-perfect feasts.

"These look pretty intense. Maybe you should try something less complicated, like a roast chicken?"

"No can do." Her high ponytail swished from side to side as she shook her head. "With his prized Chevelle in the mix, my dad was specific on the menu."

Isaiah's eyes widened as Sandra listed Stuart's requests, from the turkey basted in that sage butter seasoning to sweet potatoes and an apple-laden dessert.

"Uh-oh," he muttered.

"That about sums it up." Sandra propped her elbows on the counter and dropped her chin between her palms.

Isaiah winced. "Maybe the five dates with that Dale guy will go quickly."

As the words tumbled out of his mouth, he hoped he was long gone by the time she had to make good on the wager. They were only friends, but after last night he didn't want to think about his *friend* out with another man.

"If I'm lucky," she said, "he'll want to bring my dad along, because he's the one Dale really wants to impress."

A beep sounded and Isaiah looked at the jacket he'd draped over the other bar stool. He walked around to the side Sandra was sitting on and retrieved his phone from his jacket pocket. "Excuse me, I'm just going to take a peek at this text. Then I'll put it on silent."

Isaiah glanced down at the screen. It was a message from his father. His parents had decided to stay over in Salem for the rest of the weekend. He stared at the message and debated whether to call them.

In the end, he silenced the phone and placed it back in his jacket. His father had looked tired, but otherwise fine when his parents had left yesterday. Now he apparently felt good enough to stay over a few extra days.

Besides, Salem was just minutes away.

"You okay?"

Isaiah looked up to see Sandra staring at him, concern creasing her features. "Yeah, I'm fine."

"The expression on your face says different." She placed a hand on his forearm. "Friends, remember?"

"Friends." Isaiah nodded. He took her hand in his and sat on the stool next to her.

Smoothing a palm down his cheek, Sandra echoed his words to her moments ago. "I'm as good a listener now as I was back then."

Isaiah wasn't usually one to unburden himself to anyone, so he was surprised how easy it was to talk to her about his father's diagnosis. It was also good to know parts of their old relationship had remained intact despite time and, he thought, past hurts.

"Poor Ben. Was that text message about him? Is he in the hospital?" Sandra hit him with a barrage of questions.

Isaiah had forgotten how much Sandra had liked his father when they were dating. The feeling had been mutual, although his dad had thought they were too young to be so serious about each other at the time.

"Goodness. I can't believe you let me go on about a dumb bet when you're coming to grips with your father's cancer," she said, before he could answer any of her questions. "I'm so sorry. I never would have—"

Isaiah placed a hand on her shoulder to stop her, and then, changing his mind, pulled her into his arms instead. He kissed the top of her head. "You had no idea he was sick," he said. "Hell, I didn't either until I got home last week."

Sandra looked up, pinning him with her brown-eyed gaze. "Is he going to be okay?"

The son in him was still anxious about the strong man he'd always looked up to, but was reassured after hearing what the doctor had to say during his father's appointment earlier this week.

"I think so," Isaiah said. "They caught it early, and he completed radiation therapy yesterday. His doctor was optimistic about his prognosis."

The worry lines creasing Sandra's forehead eased as he told her about his father's epiphany and his parents spending the Halloween weekend in Salem.

"Anyway, he and my mom relived their first date last night, and today they're visiting some of the attractions they missed yesterday."

Sandra smiled, an unmistakable gleam of mischief in her eyes. "So with your folks away all weekend, what do you have planned for today?"

She stepped out of his embrace and undid the sash on her satin robe. She was naked underneath, and as beautiful as she looked with it on, he could hardly wait to strip it off.

He scooped her up into his arms and over his shoulder in one swift movement.

"Hey!" she called out, between giggles. "What are you doing?"

"First, I'm taking you back to bed." His long legs ate up in a few strides the short hallway leading to her bedroom. "Then later, I'm going to help you win your old man's Chevelle."

"Really?" Sandra asked from over his shoulder.

"Really," Isaiah confirmed, against his better judgment. "I'm going to teach you to cook, or die trying."

The next morning, Sandra rested her hand on the handle of her stocked refrigerator.

"You can do this. You can do this." She closed her eyes briefly as she repeated the mantra.

When they'd finally gotten out of bed yesterday, she and Isaiah had spent the afternoon in the housewares section of a Boston department store buying cookware. Next stop was a grocery store for basic staples, which had morphed into two full shopping carts of what Isaiah had deemed the essentials for human survival.

She glanced at the red canister on the kitchen countertop. He'd also picked up a small fire extinguisher, "just in case."

Exhaling, Sandra yanked open the fridge door. She pulled out eggs, milk and butter. During their first cooking lesson, the day before, Isaiah had suggested assembling all the ingredients before she started to cook. He'd started out simple, by demonstrating how to make the French toast they'd eaten for dinner.

Today, she was to do the actual cooking under his watchful eye.

When he'd returned to his parents' house earlier for a change of clothes, after spending a second night in her bed, Sandra decided to surprise him. She stared at the glossy picture in the cookbook of easy recipes they'd picked up during their shopping trip, and sighed. The recipe called for five minutes of prep time and ten minutes of actual cook time.

Isaiah had texted her a few moments ago; saying he was on his way back to her house. She'd have a scrumptious platter of French toast waiting when he walked through the door.

"You can do this," she whispered, forcing memories of old kitchen snafus from her head.

She turned back to the cookbook. "It's foolproof. Just like the book says."

Sandra cracked four eggs into her new mixing bowl and carefully measured out the correct amount of milk. She whisked them together and poured the results into a shallow dish.

She switched on the stove burner to melt the half stick of butter she'd already placed in the skillet. Although the recipe stated medium-high heat, Sandra lowered it to be on the safe side.

She did *not* want to screw this up.

The next step, of soaking slices of bread in the milk and eggs before transferring them to the skillet, went fairly quickly. Still, as the bread cooked, Sandra couldn't help feeling as if she'd forgotten something.

She looked at the recipe again. *Cinnamon!*

Sandra opened the cabinet door and grabbed the red spice. She quickly sprinkled a liberal amount on the sizzling bread, before flipping it with the spatula.

"Good save." She swiped the back of her hand against her forehead.

Shortly afterward, Sandra beamed down at the finished product on the kitchen island. The toast was singed in a few spots and didn't smell quite the same as Isaiah's had yesterday, but otherwise it was a pretty good effort for a beginner, she thought.

She was pulling maple syrup from the cabinet when a knock sounded at her door.

"Perfect timing." She grabbed Isaiah's hand and pulled him inside. "I've got something for you."

He waggled a brow. "Again?"

Sandra laughed and pinched his khaki-clad ass. "Later," she said. "Meanwhile, I have a surprise."

She led him into the kitchen, where her first fiasco-free meal awaited. She could barely contain her giddiness as she watched his reaction to what was essentially a meal a child could cook.

"Wow." Isaiah looked down at the plate and then scanned the kitchen.

Sandra grinned and shook her head. "No spatters. No fires. No explosion."

He wrapped an arm around her waist and pulled her to him, and she encircled hers around his neck.

"Good job." He kissed her lips. "I'm proud of you."

Sandra froze. A sense of déjà vu washed over her. He'd held her in his arms and uttered the same words the day she'd told him she'd been accepted into the summer program to study fashion design at the School of the Art Institute of Chicago.

It had all been part of their big plans for the future.

After the summer program, Isaiah was to remain in Chicago for his freshman year as an art major at the prestigious school, while she had hoped to be accepted there after finishing her senior year at Wintersage Academy.

"You okay?" he asked.

Sandra gazed up at the face of the man she knew so well, yet didn't know at all. *Friends*, she reminded herself.

And ancient hurts had no place in friendship.

"Yeah, I'm fine." She brushed off the unwanted intrusion from the past, refusing to let it ruin her morning or her accomplishment. She turned her attention to the French toast Sunday brunch awaiting them on the kitchen counter.

"I think all I ever needed cookingwise was a good teacher."

"Well, your instructor is starving." Isaiah kissed her again before releasing her from his embrace.

He chuckled and seated himself at the breakfast bar. "I never thought I'd ever say this to you, but feed me, woman."

Sandra divided the bounty between two plates and watched Isaiah smother his share in maple syrup. She picked up her fork, but placed it back on her napkin. She was too excited to eat.

She didn't want to miss Isaiah's expression after he took the first bite. His visceral reaction would tell her what words wouldn't—what he *really* thought.

Isaiah cut into the syrup-laden toast with his fork and speared a huge bite. He smiled at her before wrapping his lips around it.

Sandra didn't take her eyes off his mouth as he chewed once, then twice.

"Aargh!" His anguished cry reverberated off the walls of the small kitchen, and his eyes bulged out of his head. Tears welled in them as he hurriedly snatched his napkin.

Stunned, Sandra could only stare. She watched him cover his mouth as he undoubtedly deposited the bite into the napkin. Then he leaped from the stool, as if it were an electric chair set on sizzle, and dashed to the sink. He turned the cold water on full blast and stuck his head under the faucet.

He took several desperate slurps of cold water before coming up for air.

"Milk," he croaked.

Sandra quickly grabbed the carton of milk from the refrigerator, and Isaiah snatched it from her grasp. He turned it up to his mouth and took a long, greedy gulp.

Dozens of possibilities went through her head. Could he be allergic to one of the ingredients she'd used? She dismissed it. He'd eaten the exact same thing yesterday.

"Good Lord. What did you put in those?" Isaiah gasped after he'd finished off the carton of milk.

His face was bright red, along with his eyes, which were still tearing up.

"I—I used the same ingredients you used yesterday," she stammered.

"Show me," he said, his voice still raspy.

Sandra quickly reassembled the items on the counter. She stood by as he scanned them, before zeroing in on the small jar of cinnamon.

He picked it up and turned it around to read the label.

"What's wrong? Did the cinnamon go bad?"

A smile lit Isaiah's teary eyes, and he made a noise that sounded like a rusty chuckle. "Something like that."

He held up the jar.

This time Sandra read the label, and her stomach dropped.

"'Cayenne pepper.'" She reread the words aloud and then remembered hastily grabbing the seasoning after she'd initially forgotten to add it to the toast.

She touched her fingertips to Isaiah's mouth. "You poor baby. I'm so sorry."

He pursed his lips in an awkward attempt to kiss her fingers. "It was just a little mix-up," he said. The bright red blanketing his features had abated, but his eyes were still watery.

He opened the cabinet, pulled out the real cinnamon and compared the two. Both small glass jars were the same size, and the labels were the same color.

"The pepper is a shade or two brighter, but I can see where someone could easily get them mixed up," Isaiah said.

Sandra shook her head. She'd been so careful, yet she'd still managed to screw everything up.

"My dad was right," she said. "Mason knows his way around a kitchen better than I do. I need to call off this stupid bet right now, before I inadvertently poison my entire family."

She turned to leave the kitchen. She was calling her father right now, and this time she wasn't going to let her pride stop her from pulling out of their wager. Even if it meant having to endure five miserable evenings of Dale's company.

Isaiah took ahold of her arm. "It was an oversight, Sandra." His long fingers slid downward until he was holding her hand. "No real harm done."

She swiped away a stray tear leaking from his eyes with the pad of her thumb. "How can you say that after I—" she began.

Isaiah answered the question before she could finish it. "Because I believe in you." His voice still held a raspy edge from the pepper. "Once you put your mind to something, anything, there's nothing you can't do. You were the one who got us both through trigonometry. You also rescued my sophomore year science project, remember?"

Sandra nodded as she recalled helping collect and

analyze data. "How microwave radiation affects different organisms," she said.

"You didn't blow up the microwave then, did you?"

"We were nuking radish seeds. If it had been something edible it would have been a different story."

This morning's incident proved just how inept she was in the kitchen. Yet Isaiah had her almost believing.

No. She shook her head.

"I appreciate the kind words and you trying to teach me to cook, but we both know there's no way I'll be good enough to prepare a big meal like Thanksgiving dinner in three and a half weeks. Besides, my business is hopping with the holiday season coming up. Not to mention the outcome of Tuesday's election…" Her voice drifted off as she recalled how busy the next two months would be for her. It had been a huge mistake to allow herself to be goaded into the bet in the first place.

"Look at me." Isaiah used his forefinger to tilt her chin upward until their gazes connected. "I have a pretty good idea this wager isn't really about cooking a meal, right?"

Sandra didn't answer. As she met his intense stare, it was if he was peering into her very soul.

"You still feel like you have something to prove, don't you?"

Although it wasn't necessary, Sandra answered his question with a single bob of her head. She swallowed hard as she realized time and distance hadn't broken their special bond. A connection deeper than physical attraction, more intimate than sex.

Isaiah Jacobs still knew her inside out, better than she knew herself.

"I'm your friend. What's important to you is important to me," he said.

Moreover, he seemed to really care, Sandra thought.

"I'm no chef," Isaiah continued. "I've never attempted a Thanksgiving spread, either. But I can find my way around a kitchen, and if you really want to win this bet, I'll do whatever I can to help."

She stared up at him as he spoke.

"We're both college-educated adults. Between the two of us we should be able to follow a few recipes and ensure you get dinner on the table."

"One of the terms of the wager is that I do it myself."

Isaiah nodded. "And you will."

"Exactly what are you proposing?" Sandra asked.

A confident smile spread across his lips. "That we handle this situation military style."

Sandra frowned. "So what are you going to do, bark orders at me?"

Shaking his head, Isaiah chuckled. "Not at all," he said. "Sure, discipline is part of military training, but it's only one aspect. Another is learning by rote. Doing something repeatedly until it becomes routine."

Sandra found herself smiling back at him as understanding dawned. "You're saying we'll do it over and over again."

"Until you can prepare Thanksgiving dinner in your sleep," Isaiah finished. "We both have to eat, anyway. We'll simply cook Thanksgiving dishes for dinner every night."

Sandra closed her eyes briefly to consider it. He'd made the solution to the problem complicating her life all week seem almost simple. The man also made her feel as if she could accomplish anything.

So maybe it could work, Sandra thought. She did have something to prove, and dammit, *she wanted to win*.

Unfortunately, her common sense took the opportunity to pay her another visit. It carried a huge banner with the word *DANGER* scrawled across it in big red letters.

If you're not careful, you'll fall for him again, and just like last time, he'll break your heart.

Sandra brushed aside the warning call. That wasn't going to happen.

All Isaiah was offering, all she wanted from him, was friendship and help in the kitchen. Sex hotter than her cayenne-infused French toast was just a bonus.

Besides, he'd be gone the day after Thanksgiving. What could it hurt? She'd win the bet and have fun in the process.

"Okay, let's do it," she said.

"Good," Isaiah said. "All I ask is one thing."

Sandra raised a brow. "And what's that?"

"I want to be the first person you take for a ride as the new owner of your old man's Chevelle."

"Deal." Sandra held out her hand to seal their agreement with a handshake.

Isaiah regarded her extended hand. "Oh, I think we can do better than a handshake," he said. "A lot better."

Sandra grinned and inclined her head toward the abandoned French toast. "Perhaps seconds on my red-hot cooking?"

"Later," he said, desire simmering in his dark-eyed gaze. He pulled her to him. The hard evidence of what he had in mind pressed against her. "First, I need to satisfy a craving for your red-hot loving."

Chapter 9

Sunrise found Isaiah seated on a craggy cliff overlooking the rocks and sandy coastline hugging the deep blue waters of the Atlantic.

The air was crisp and carried the salty tang of the ocean. A smell that was unmistakably home.

He inhaled a big gulp of it, and as he exhaled he knew the air was also tinged with an intangible he couldn't smell.

Independence.

This morning he'd awakened to his own body clock. Later, he'd eat when he was hungry, sleep when he was tired, jump in his old truck and drive as far as he wanted without a schedule, an order to follow or restrictions.

Or maybe he'd simply spend the rest of the day sitting on this rock, painting.

He studied the sunlight glistening off the waves as

the tide swept across the sand. He looked down at the page in his sketchbook where he'd attempted to capture the subtle magnificence in watercolor.

The small ring-bound book, or one similar to it, had been his constant companion over the years. He could hardly wait to finally have a studio he could fill with giant canvases.

Soon, he thought.

Isaiah exchanged the short pencil for a watercolor brush and began filling in the sparkling blue of the ocean in short, quick strokes. He was so engrossed in his work, he didn't hear Sandra approach from behind.

"Morning."

Isaiah turned at the sound of her voice. She stood behind him dressed in sneakers, black running tights and a red fleece jacket. A red headband held her shoulder-length hair off her face. She looked adorable.

He put his sketchbook aside and stood. "Morning, gorgeous." He kissed her. The feel of her lips against his reminded him how good it had felt to wake up beside her the past three mornings.

Too good.

Now that the weekend was over, he'd have to get used to sleeping in his own bed, alone.

"I wondered where you'd gone off to," Sandra said. "When I woke up, you weren't in bed, but your truck was still parked outside."

Isaiah looked up at the sun and then at the beach below them. "When I was away, this is the scene that came to mind whenever I thought of Wintersage. I wanted to see if I could do it justice."

Sandra glanced at the small sketchbook and the portable paint palette on the cliff ledge. "Can I see?"

"I don't want to hold you up from your run," he said.

She shook her head. "I'm not a runner. I just do a half hour walk along the beach weekday mornings so I can indulge in a cupcake for lunch. Oh, the bakery has a new owner. You should stop in while you're here, her cupcakes are—"

"Positively addictive," Isaiah interrupted. "I went there for the first time a week ago, and I'm already a regular customer."

"Well, let me take a peek at your watercolor."

Isaiah took her hand to steady her as she sat down on the large rock, and then took a seat beside her. He passed her the sketchbook and waited, eager to hear her opinion. Just as he used to do when they were students at Wintersage Academy.

She took her time examining the unfinished painting, which was the size of a large snapshot. Then she looked out onto the water and back to his work.

"It's beautiful, Isaiah. You're not even done, and already it's better than the real thing." She inclined her head toward the sketchbook in her hands. "May I?"

Isaiah nodded. He watched her go back to the worn front cover of the book and begin flipping pages. She stopped at his rendition of the Tower of Palazzo Vecchio in Italy.

"You were in Florence?" she asked.

"After Annapolis, I was stationed in Italy."

"I had no idea." Sandra studied the painting, before flipping over to a landscape that included Mount Etna shortly after one of the volcano's famous eruptions. "I've seen your parents over the years, and I've designed dresses for your mother, but we always tiptoed around the subject of you." Sandra shrugged. "I guess I always assumed you were on a warship somewhere."

"The navy puts their personnel where they're most needed, and they determined that, as an economics major, I was needed pushing paper in a comptroller's office at a naval air base in Sicily," he said.

She continued to look through the sketchbook. "So this is what you did when you weren't helping keep track of the navy's dollars?"

Isaiah nodded. "This and spending any downtime at art museums in Italy and the rest of Europe."

She returned the book to him. "I didn't realize you were still an artist."

Isaiah nodded. "I'm as passionate about it as I was back in school."

"It's a shame you didn't pursue it full-time," she said softly. "Who knows what you could have accomplished by now."

An awkward silence ensued as the part of their past they'd been careful to avoid took up residence between them.

Silence and regret.

"It's the reason I'm booked on a flight to London the day after Thanksgiving," Isaiah said finally.

Sandra gazed at him, a questioning expression on her face.

He gathered up the portable items that made up his makeshift art studio and nudged her with his elbow. "Let's walk, and I'll update you."

He stood, extended his free hand to Sandra and led her down the path of the cliff walk and through a bed of rocks to the wet sand. Although there was no real need, he continued to hold her hand as they started their trek down the stretch of beach.

"I was accepted at the Royal Academy of Arts," he said. "Classes don't start until January, but I want to give myself time to settle in, find studio space and a place to live."

Sandra didn't speak immediately, but he felt a hitch in her stride.

"Wow. I mean, congratulations," she said. "That school tops most lists of the best art schools in the world. They must have been really impressed with your work."

Isaiah nodded. He hadn't had many pieces when he'd applied, because of restrictions on his time. He'd been overjoyed to make the cut and to be able to finance a few years off to study on his own.

Despite his wealthy background and substantial inheritances left to him by his grandparents, he'd lived frugally during his stint in the navy, putting aside money every pay period to finance his dreams with an income he'd earned.

Sandra looked up at him. "I'm happy for you," she said. "But to be honest, I'm also surprised. I know you said you were leaving, but in the back of my mind I figured you'd end up—"

"Going to work at Martine's," he finished.

She shoved her free hand into her jacket pocket. "After all, it was part of your parents' master plan for you."

Isaiah listened for traces of lingering anger or bitterness in her tone. There were none. Only a barely detectable hint of sadness rode the salty air.

"You even majored in economics at the naval academy, just like they wanted."

Insisted was more like it, he thought. She was right. He'd followed their blueprint to the letter.

Until now.

"I'm sorry, Sandra," Isaiah said. She hadn't asked for an apology, but he owed her the words that already were ten years overdue. "I know I—"

Sandra stopped walking. She touched her fingertips to his lips and shook her head. A woman with gray hair walking a golden retriever bobbed her head in greeting as she passed them.

"An apology isn't necessary," Sandra said. "We were both kids, and it was a very long time ago. You made the best decision you could at the time."

I made the wrong one.

"Doesn't matter now, anyway," Sandra said, as if she'd heard the words echoing through his head. "Friends, remember?"

"Friends." He squeezed the hand he still held, and they resumed walking.

"You're only here for a few weeks, and I'm not interested in drudging up old drama. Let's just enjoy each other's company," she said.

Now it was Isaiah's turn to be surprised. He hadn't come across many women who hadn't wanted to talk, dissect every problem and then rehash it ad nauseam. The more he got to know this Sandra, the more she intrigued him.

"I'd like that," he said.

She stopped again. "Speaking of parents, I think it would be best if we were discreet about our *friendship*," she said. "We don't want them jumping to all the wrong conclusions."

"You're right, but I'm sure the brief conversation we

had at the Halloween party has already hit the Winter-sage gossip circuit."

"And been blown totally out of proportion," Sandra added.

She looked up at the sun and then back to her house.

"I'm keeping you, aren't I?" Isaiah asked. "The weekend has been great, but I'm sure you've got to get back to work this morning."

Actually, great was an understatement, he thought. It had been incredible. Given him a new reason to loathe Mondays. And it wasn't just the sex. He was enjoying getting to know the person she'd become.

Isaiah liked all-grown-up Sandra, *a lot*.

"I do have a ton of work to do." She gnawed at her bottom lip, drawing his attention to her sexy mouth and the lips he could kiss for days without stopping to breathe.

He forced himself to focus on what she was saying instead of the tightening in his groin.

"But Mondays are my creative days, and I sometimes work from home."

Sandra gazed up at the sky again and out at the horizon. "I was just thinking. Maybe I could pop up to the house for a quick shower and a thermos of coffee, and then join you out here to sketch out a few preliminary designs while you paint."

Isaiah flashed back to them sitting on the cliffs overlooking this same beach after school. He'd be drawing, while Sandra sat beside him sketching a dress design she was positive was destined for the Paris runway.

"Just like old times." They said the words at the same time.

Isaiah looked up toward her house. "Want some company in that shower?"

A slow, sexy smile spread over lips that were wreaking havoc on his imagination and a certain hard part of his anatomy. "I can't think of a better way to start the week."

That evening, Sandra arrived at The Quarterdeck to find her friends already seated.

She grinned at the sight of Janelle, delighted to see her friend and eager to hear about her honeymoon in paradise. She gave both her and Vicki quick hugs and then slid into the empty chair at the table.

"Looking good, *Mrs. Dubois*," Sandra said, emphasizing Janelle's new title. She took a quick sip of the drink her friends had already ordered for her. "If you've started telling Vicki about Tahiti, you'll just have to start over," she said. "I want to hear every detail."

Instead of launching into the gushing honeymoon report Sandra anticipated, Janelle stared at her wordlessly. Her friend's suspicion-filled eyes narrowed.

"What?" Sandra asked.

Janelle looked her up and down. "That's what I'm trying to put my finger on."

Sandra scrunched her face in confusion. "Sounds like you may have brought home a case of jet lag along with your gorgeous, sun-kissed skin."

Leaning back in her chair, Janelle ran a red-nailed fingertip along the edge of her martini glass and continued to study her. "So-o-o, if I'm the one who just returned from her honeymoon, how come *you're* the one glowing?"

Sandra coughed, nearly choking on her drink. "D-don't be silly," she sputtered.

"You look like you just walked in from a weekend sex retreat."

Sandra watched her two best friends exchange glances.

"I'm sure it's no coincidence Isaiah Jacobs is back in town." Vicki kicked into the conversation. "He and Sandra were spotted at the rec center Friday night looking mighty cozy."

"How'd you know he…" Sandra began.

"Wintersage is a small town," Janelle stated.

Sandra groaned inwardly. Usually, she didn't hold out on her two best friends. It was just she knew they'd immediately jump to conclusions and read more into what was going on between her and Isaiah than was there.

"You two are imagining things." She turned to Vicki in hopes of jump-starting a change in topic. "So did you come up with any ideas for your big makeover?"

"What makeover?" Janelle asked.

The waiter dropped off a basket of piping hot bread at their table and took their dinner orders. Sandra requested the native shrimp and immediately reached for a roll. She was starved.

Besides, the sooner they started stuffing their mouths with food, the better.

"So what's this about a makeover?" Janelle asked again.

Vicki shrugged. "It's nothing. I'm just contemplating a few changes." She turned to Sandra. "Now back to you."

"It's obvious you slept with him, so just admit it," Janelle said.

Vicki took a sip of her white wine spritzer. "Yeah, you'll feel better."

If Sandra had known it was that obvious, she would have covered her so-called glow with a coating of makeup. *No use trying to deny it now*, she thought, and confirmed their suspicions with a nod of her head.

"I knew it." Janelle flashed Vicki a knowing look.

"Ha! You should have heard her last week, before she knew he was in town," Vicki said. She fisted her hands on her hips and began a spot-on imitation of Sandra's voice. "'Isaiah was just a high school sweetheart. I think about him as much as I do Mrs. Sterling's chemistry class or after-school cheerleader practice, which is never.'"

Janelle snorted. "She did a lot more than think about him."

Sandra ate her bread while her friends continued to talk about her as if she wasn't sitting with them.

"She brushed me off as some kind of romantic sap when I told her I always thought they'd end up together," Vicki said. "I know a happily-ever-after in the making when I see one."

Swallowing the last of her bread, Sandra held up her hands in a halting motion. "Whoa, slow down, the both of you."

This was exactly why she hadn't planned on confiding to them or anyone that she'd had sex with Isaiah. *And boy, had she ever, over and over again.* Sandra shoved aside the illicit images the weekend had left imprinted on her brain.

"Isaiah and I are not dating. We are not a couple. We're simply old friends," she said.

Vicki opened her mouth, but Sandra cut her off, determined to put a stop to any talk of romance before it started.

"Friends," she reiterated.

Janelle winked at Vicki. "Yeah, Ballard and I were friends in Tahiti, too." She raised her martini glass and clinked it against Vicki's wineglass.

"Really close friends," Vicki added.

"Friends that get naked." Janelle turned her attention back to Sandra. "Just like you and Isaiah."

Rolling her eyes skyward, Sandra shook her head. "You two are a mess." She craned her neck and looked around the restaurant's dining room in search of their waiter. "Where is our food, anyway? You two need something to occupy your mouths other than my business."

Janelle held up a finger. "Just one question."

Sandra sighed. "Okay, go ahead."

"Was the sex worth the ten-year wait?"

Both she and Vicki leaned in, awaiting her reply, and Sandra couldn't hold back the smile she knew was spreading across her lips.

"Hell, yes!"

The three of them were laughing when the waiter arrived with their entrées. As they dug into their seafood dishes, often sampling from each other's plates, Janelle filled them in on her tropical honeymoon and first days of marital bliss with Ballard.

Janelle was still talking all things marriage when their plates had been cleared, and the waiter returned with a huge slice of chocolate cake and three forks.

"It all sounds so romantic." Vicki cut into the layers of chocolate and frosting with her fork, but her eyes were on Janelle. "Why didn't you stay longer?"

"We wanted to stay at least another week, but I needed to be back in time for Election Day tomorrow," she said. "The polls are still showing Oliver Windom running ahead of my dad." Janelle glanced at her gold wristwatch. "In fact, I probably should be going soon. I'm still jet-lagged, and I want to be at Dad's campaign headquarters bright and early tomorrow morning to start working the phones."

Sandra fell silent. Jordan's calculations had the election close, but tilting in Windom's favor. So far, she'd managed to stay neutral in the politics that landed her brother and her best friend on opposite sides, and she planned on keeping it that way.

Besides, she had a personal interest in tomorrow's election that had nothing to do with the highly publicized Ballard-Windom race. Sandra would be keeping a close eye on the returns in the Massachusetts governor's race.

Depending on how it turned out, she might have the honor of dressing the state's first lady for the gubernatorial inaugural ball.

The aroma of tonight's macrobiotic meal selection greeted Isaiah as he walked through the back door of his parents' house.

Oh, hell no.

Hoping they hadn't heard him come in, he took a step backward in hopes of quietly easing undetected out the same door he'd just come through.

"Isaiah," his father called out.

Groaning inwardly, Isaiah closed the door behind him.

Sure enough, his mother was bringing one of the

delivered meals to the table. He glanced at the serving platter. The food on it was brown, apparently a bean and grain dish, smothered in seasonal autumn vegetables. It looked about as appetizing as his shoe.

"Just in time for dinner." A smirk accompanied Ben's words.

"Um, no thanks," Isaiah said quickly.

"Oh, come on." His father's cajoling tone belied the devilish gleam in his eyes.

Isaiah spared the meal another glance. "I'm not hungry."

"Nonsense." His father kicked the empty chair from under the table with his foot, and the chair legs scraped against the floor. "Surely, you can sit down to a *delicious* family dinner with your sweet mama and sickly old dad."

Isaiah shot him a laser-beam side-eye, and Ben coughed for effect.

"It would be nice for the three of us to have dinner together," his mother said. "After all, you're only going to be with us for a few more weeks."

Isaiah sighed. He'd missed them, too. Still, as he washed his hands and took the chair his father had pushed out for him, he wished they were sitting down to a meal of steaks off the grill.

Cecily heaped a serving of the entrée onto her husband's plate and set it in front of him. She then did the same for Isaiah, before serving herself.

"Thanks, Mom." The manners drilled into him by his parents and the military automatically kicked in. Isaiah stared down at the mound of brown with steam curling off it and tried to think of something nice to say. "Um…it looks…"

"Like a pile of horseshit," his father declared.

The boisterous laughter of the Jacobs men filled the kitchen, both oblivious to the frown on the face of the family matriarch.

"Lord, it's like sitting at the table with two little boys," Cecily huffed, when the laughter died down to snickers. "You two haven't even tried it."

She looked expectantly from her husband to her son. "It's packed with nutrients and is good for us."

Isaiah picked up his fork and poked at the food on the plate. His father nudged him with an elbow. "You heard your mother. Eat up, boy. It's good for you," he said.

"Why don't you set an example and eat yours first," Isaiah countered.

The two laughed again, and this time Cecily was unable to resist joining in.

"We're *all* going to eat it," she said, then shoveled a forkful into her mouth.

Isaiah and his father reluctantly followed suit. It wasn't much on taste, but Isaiah had no complaints about the company. He listened as his parents filled him in on their weekend. The two of them had essentially gone only a few miles up the road, but it appeared to have done them a lot of good.

Ben still looked tired, but Isaiah was heartened to see that the fine lines and dark circles around his eyes seemed to have diminished since he'd last seen him on Friday. In fact, both his parents appeared to be in great spirits.

"Glad you two had a fun weekend," Isaiah said.

"We did," they stated simultaneously, exchanging glances.

His father cleared his throat. "Actually, there's something we need to talk to you about."

A sense of unease came over Isaiah, dampening what up until now had been a pleasant evening. The last time his father had said those words had been over a week ago, when he'd broken the news of his prostate cancer diagnosis.

Ben reached across the table and took his wife's hand. Isaiah looked at their laced fingers. While he knew his parents loved each other, he'd rarely seen displays of affection between them when he'd been growing up.

In some ways, they'd seemed more like business partners than man and wife. Most of their conversations and activities had centered on Martine's Fine Furnishings.

"Your father and I have decided to sell the company," his mother said.

Stunned, Isaiah stared at them, dumbfounded, looking from one to the other. "What?"

"We made the decision over the weekend, son," his father said.

"I—I don't understand."

They both were absolutely devoted to the company, which had been in his mother's family for generations. All his life, Martine's had been their top priority.

His mother said pretty much the same thing as she began to explain her reasons for selling. "This weekend gave your father and me time to do some soul-searching," she said. "We've made the business our entire life at the expense of each other and you."

Ben nodded, still holding his wife's hand. "We're fortunate the cancer was caught in the early stages, and my prognosis is excellent. Still, facing your mortality crystalizes what's important and what's no longer worth your time."

Trying to absorb the news, Isaiah turned to his mother. "But just the other night you were on my case about duty and legacy."

"I only told you what your grandfather told me when he put me in charge of Martine's," she said. "I devoted a good chunk of my life to that company. So has your father."

Her features softened as she smiled at her husband. "From now on my duty is to my marriage and you. I'll fulfill the Martine legacy by making sure the company goes to a buyer prepared to take it into the future."

"Sounds like your minds are made up," Isaiah said.

His mother nodded. "We've already set the wheels in motion and hope to find a buyer soon."

Isaiah's eyes rounded. "That was fast."

Cecily laughed. "Now that we've made the decision to put it up for sale, we can't get rid of it soon enough. We're looking forward to spending some time together."

"That's where you come in, son," Ben said. "We have a favor to ask of you."

"What do you need?"

They exchanged glances before his mother spoke. "Your father and I would like you to keep an eye on things at Martine's."

Isaiah began to shake his head, until his father interjected, "Only temporarily, while you're in town. This isn't some trick to try to shackle you to the company or Wintersage," he quickly explained. "I just don't want to wait until we find a buyer to take my favorite girl out for some fun."

"He's talking about going to Disney World," his mother said with a giggle.

A giggle. His mother never giggled.

At the sound of it, Isaiah could only nod his head. He had the next two years to immerse himself in his art. Meanwhile, his parents' ecstatic expressions were worth a few short weeks of his time.

Chapter 10

Sandra switched off the overhead track lights at Swoon Couture at four o'clock on the dot and bounded down the staircase of the Victorian.

"Where are you off to so fast?" Vicki stood at the entrance to Petals on the first floor, holding a bunch of purple and yellow New England aster blooms in her hand. She leaned against the doorjamb, eyes narrowed. "I know Janelle took off for Election Day to help her dad, but you usually don't leave until at least seven."

"I need to vote, and then swing by the grocery store."

Hit by a sudden wave of paranoia, Sandra opened her red leather bag and shifted through its contents. She found her shopping list in the bag's front pocket and breathed a sigh of relief.

"Grocery store? Why in the world would you..." Vicki stopped midsentence, and her jaw dropped as realization dawned. "You didn't call off the bet with your father, did you?"

Sandra shook her head slowly. She watched her friend's eyes roll toward the ceiling.

"For goodness' sakes, why not? We both know there's no way you'll win."

A few days ago, Sandra had felt the same way. Only one thing had changed.

Isaiah.

He'd had her believing just maybe she could win. Her mind conjured up an image of the two of them taking the Chevelle out for a spin after she won the bet. With the wind in their faces and an endless open road before them, just like that day he'd gotten his driver's license and taken her for a ride in his truck.

A shiver shimmied down her back at the thought of him, and the fact that she'd be seeing him tonight.

"What are you grinning about?"

Vicki's question snapped her out of her thoughts. Sandra avoided her friend's assessing eyes. "I am not grinning."

"Next you're going to tell me it has nothing to do with your *friend* Isaiah," she said.

Sandra shrugged. "He's helping me learn my way around the kitchen so I can win the bet, that's all."

Vicki snorted and shook her head. "Then you'd better stop by the store's pharmacy aisle to pick up something for upset stomach," she said. "Isaiah may not be your knight in shining armor, but he'll need a stomach made of armor if he's foolish enough to eat your cooking."

Sandra opened her mouth to protest, but thought of the cayenne-pepper incident and snapped it shut. As she pushed open the front door of the Victorian, Vicki called out to her, "Be careful!"

"I'll try not to burn my house down," Sandra joked in reply.

"I'm not talking about cooking." Her friend's tone turned serious. "I'm talking about with your heart."

Sandra had shoved Vicki's unnecessary warning aside by the time she unlocked her front door a short while later, juggling a purse and grocery sacks. She dumped the bags on the breakfast bar and hung her coat in the closet.

Isaiah had called a few minutes before, saying he was driving over. She resisted the urge to run a brush through her hair, apply a fresh coat of lip gloss and spritz on some perfume.

You're just friends, Sandra silently reminded herself, thinking back to Vicki's warning.

Sure, an undeniable physical attraction had always existed between them, she thought. However, unlike when they were teenagers, they'd acted on it *often* in the past few days. She was certain they'd have worked it out of their systems long before it was time for him to leave for London.

Shortly afterward, Sandra opened the door to Isaiah, surprised to see him wearing a dark cashmere overcoat instead of his leather jacket.

Before she could say hello, he pulled her into his embrace.

"I missed you last night." His deep baritone made her body go all tingly and gooseflesh rise on the back of her neck.

Sandra braced her palms against his coat, which still

held the night chill. She inhaled the faint smell of mint on his breath before he captured her mouth in a kiss.

She'd missed him, too.

Isaiah held her close, and his tongue stroked hers in a long, leisurely kiss that left her breathless. Afterward, he touched his forehead to hers. "You ready to cook?" he asked.

Sandra nodded and reluctantly peeled herself off him. Getting busy in the kitchen was the last thing on her mind, unless it involved them naked and figuring out a better use for her kitchen counter.

Isaiah shrugged off his coat. Underneath he wore a navy business suit in a slim European cut that made his wide shoulders look even broader and his abs appear even flatter than the six-pack she'd trailed her tongue down yesterday afternoon.

Sandra's mouth went dry at the thought. She watched him loosen the knot on the tie, before shedding it and the suit jacket.

"You're looking good tonight," she said.

It was an understatement. He looked sexy as hell in a suit, she thought, watching him roll up the sleeves on his white dress shirt.

"I spent the day working at Martine's," he said.

"Really?" Sandra dragged her gaze away from the corded muscle of his forearms.

Isaiah blew out a weary sigh. "Not permanently, just while I'm in town."

Sandra only nodded as they made their way to the kitchen.

"I know what you're thinking. That it's some kind of ploy on my folks' part to suck me into running the family business."

"It did cross my mind."

"I initially thought the same thing." Isaiah dried his hands on a paper towel after washing them at the sink. "But they're putting the business up for sale."

"You're kidding!" Sandra looked up from the ingredients she was assembling on the counter.

She and Isaiah had already decided on tonight's menu of a green salad and pan-seared chicken breasts. They were working on holiday side dishes first, and this evening they'd planned to tackle stuffing.

After combing through the cookbooks, Sandra had found a recipe for a skillet apple stuffing. She figured it would be the best way to cover her father's Thanksgiving dinner requests of stuffing and something with apples in one dish. He had said he wasn't picky.

Isaiah filled her in on the details of his parents' decision to sell the company that had been in his mother's family for generations, as they stood side by side at the kitchen counter doing the prep work for the stuffing. He chopped apples, while Sandra cut baguettes into one-inch chunks.

"You should have seen them." Isaiah slid the bread she'd chopped into the oven. "They seemed so…I don't know, like a huge burden had been taken off their shoulders."

"Yours, too," Sandra said. "You can go to London free of a guilt trip for not working at the family business."

They exchanged a glance of mutual understanding.

Isaiah crossed his arms and leaned against the counter as they waited for the bread to toast. "I guess I'm not the only one who's had to deal with that particular monkey on their back," he said. "Your father didn't exactly encourage you to become a designer."

"That's an understatement," she said. "Nothing would make him happier than for me to close Swoon Couture and go to work at Woolcott Industries."

"You know, we've spent so much time talking about our family businesses, we haven't talked much about yours."

Sandra raised a brow. "We don't spend a lot of time talking," she teased.

"Can I help it if you can't keep your hands off me?" Isaiah wrapped an arm around her waist and tugged her to him.

She'd licked her lips in anticipation of his kiss when the timer on the oven chimed.

Isaiah brushed his lips against hers in the briefest, sweetest of kisses. "Later," he promised.

A promise she could hardly wait for him to deliver on.

He slowly released her, and Sandra wished dinner had a fast-forward button and they could speed through it straight to her bedroom. She sighed as she watched him bend over to pull the baking sheet from the stove. The man had an incredible ass.

"Eyes on the recipe," Isaiah said, his back to her.

"How'd you know I was…"

"I can feel you."

Sandra thought back to Halloween night, when she, too, had felt his eyes on her body as if they'd been his hands. She felt a sudden rush of heat that had nothing to do with the open oven door.

Tonight couldn't come soon enough.

Isaiah took over reading the recipe aloud as Sandra

followed his instructions. They kept their conversation to a minimum, allowing her to focus solely on preparing the meal. Isaiah intervened only to double-check the spices and make sure the paprika was indeed paprika, not cayenne pepper.

It was after seven when they finally sat down at her dining table to eat. A bouquet of bright yellow sunflowers, which she'd brought home from Petals last week, adorned the glossy black tabletop, adding an air of festiveness to the meal.

"Well, it certainly appears delicious," Isaiah said.

Sandra picked up her fork and poked at the stuffing. She had to admit it did look pretty good. However, given her history, who knew what it would taste like?

Isaiah fearlessly took a huge bite of stuffing. Sandra stared across the table as he chewed, half expecting him to spit it right back out.

A slow smile spread over his face, and he nodded. "Go on, try it." He helped himself to more.

Sandra lifted her fork to her mouth and took a tentative bite. The savory flavor of seasoned bread tinged with apple sweetness flooded her taste buds.

"It's good!" she said, excited. "It's really good."

Isaiah confirmed it by digging enthusiastically into his plate. Sandra joined him, relishing every single bite.

"Congratulations. I believe you've officially broken your kitchen jinx," he said after dinner, as they made quick work of the kitchen cleanup.

"I wouldn't go that far, but I agree tonight was a good start." Sandra rested a palm on his forearm. "Thank you. I couldn't have done it without you."

He placed his hand over hers. "Yeah, you could have. You've grown into an amazing woman, Sandra. I don't think there's anything you can't accomplish," he said. "I'm just glad we have this opportunity to get to know each other again."

She swallowed the lump of emotion rising in her throat. As she met his intense gaze, Vicki's warning to guard her heart sounded in her head. Sandra averted her eyes to pull herself together.

Friends, she reminded herself. It was what they *both* wanted. Also, at this stage in their lives it was what they both needed.

"Me, too," she said.

Catching a glimpse of the time on the microwave clock, Sandra remembered the election.

"The polls are closing." She scooted out of the kitchen into the living room to turn on the flat-screen television anchored above the fireplace. "The election returns should start coming in soon."

"You're caught up in all the hubbub surrounding the big Howerton-Windom race, too?" Isaiah sat beside her on the black-and-white graphic print sofa.

Sandra flipped the channels on the remote until she came to a local station broadcasting election coverage.

"Not me," she said, "but Jordan's running Oliver Windom's campaign."

Isaiah lifted a brow. "Is that awkward for you, being such good friends with Janelle?"

Sandra shook her head. "Not really. Neither of them ever asked who I'd planned to vote for, and I didn't volunteer the information."

"Smart thinking."

"I'm not about to let politics get in the way of a life-long friendship or my relationship with my big brother." Sandra eyed the incoming vote tallies scrolling across the bottom of the television screen. "Besides, the governor's race is the one I'm interested in."

"What issue are you concerned with?"

Sandra liked the way he leaned forward and focused all his attention on her. It had always been that way with Isaiah. Everything in his body language conveyed that he genuinely cared about her thoughts, her feelings and what she had to say.

"Actually, my reason is going to sound pretty selfish, considering serious problems across the state like unemployment, education and the environment, just to name a few," she said. "And believe it or not, I would have voted for him, anyway."

Isaiah touched a hand to her knee. "No judgment from me. I was just curious."

Sandra inclined her head toward the television, where one of the candidates for governor was being interviewed at his campaign headquarters. "If he wins, I'm on the short list to design his wife's gown for the inaugural ball."

After the interview, the reporter announced that both the Howerton-Windom and the race for governor were too close to call. "The tallies are coming in, but it's going to be a long night."

Isaiah rose from the sofa, yawned and stretched.

"You leaving?" Sandra asked, disappointed. However, she understood he'd had a long day.

"With you having a shot a designing a gown that would be seen statewide, or maybe even nationally? You're kidding, right?" he replied. "I'm headed to the kitchen to put on a pot of coffee. I want to be wide-awake to see how this turns out for you."

As Sandra watched him walk into the kitchen, something else Vicki had said came to mind.

"Prince Charming won't divert you from your goals...he'll want to be there to cheer you on..."

Two cups of coffee and a bowl of popcorn later, Isaiah watched the election coverage on television with a sleeping Sandra snuggled against him on the sofa.

The Howerton-Windom race had been called over an hour ago, with Darren Howerton declared the winner. However, Isaiah didn't disturb Sandra with the news, deciding to wait until a winner in the governor's race had been announced.

As she slept, he studied her flawless dark skin, unable to find words to describe its luminous glow. It was as if crushed diamonds shimmered beneath its rich mahogany tones. He didn't want to disturb her rest, but he couldn't resist smoothing the back of his hand down her satiny cheek.

God, he loved looking at her.

Loved.

What the hell? Isaiah blinked hard, pushing away the errant thought and snapping the spell the woman in his arms had managed to cast over him in her sleep.

He glanced around her cozy, comfortable little house.

It was a little too cozy, and he was becoming way too comfortable here and with its owner.

You're friends, Isaiah reminded himself.

The sex? It was simply a novelty they'd get out of their systems soon enough. He likened it to kids who'd been denied their favorite ice cream and then suddenly were allowed to eat as much as they'd wanted, as often as they liked.

Eventually, they'd tire of it, he reasoned, because even the sweetest, most decadent treat got old after you overindulged.

Isaiah stole another look at her, closed his eyes briefly and exhaled.

In a parallel universe this would have been his life.

He and Sandra would have spent the evening cooking dinner together and talking about their workday. They might have gone for a walk on the beach after dinner or snuggled up on the sofa, just as she was doing now. Later, he'd have taken her not to her bed, but *their* bed, where he would have made love to her deep into the night.

Isaiah glanced around the chicly decorated living room. As relaxed as he felt here, it wasn't his home. Sandra wasn't his, either. He'd forfeited his right to both when he'd done what he believed was his duty instead of following his heart.

Now he and Sandra were at different stages in life.

She was already living her dream and doing exactly what she'd set out to do back in high school. Meanwhile, he was still reaching for his, which meant he would be on that flight to London the day after Thanksgiving— no matter what.

Isaiah gently removed his arm from around Sandra and stood. He stretched and stifled a yawn with his fist.

"And in the governor's race…"

His ears perked up and he turned toward the television.

"We're just moments away from declaring a winner," the news anchor said.

Isaiah leaned over a sleeping Sandra and nudged her. "Wake up, baby." The endearment slipped out as if he'd been calling her it for years.

She looked up at him, blinking away sleep.

"They're about to call the governor's race," he said.

Sandra pushed off the sofa and looked up at the television. Isaiah saw her gnaw at her bottom lip and reached for her hand.

"And now let's go live to the headquarters of Massachusetts' new governor-elect," the news anchor said.

Seconds later, Sandra's candidate appeared on the screen.

"He won!" She dropped Isaiah's hand and wrapped her arms around his neck.

He lifted her until her feet dangled off the floor, and planted a kiss on her lips. "Congratulations."

She slid down the length of his body as he lowered her back to the ground.

"Well, this is just the first hurdle," she said, bracing her hands on his biceps. "I've sketched out a few ideas, but I still have to decide on one to send his wife. Also, she mentioned considering a few Boston-based designers who are very talented."

Isaiah dropped a kiss on the top of Sandra's head. "I'm sure whatever you submit will be her top pick."

Sandra laughed and playfully slapped at his arm. "And what makes you so sure?" she asked. "You haven't seen a dress I designed since high school."

He looked over her head and let his eyes wander around their surroundings again. The bold black-and-white would have been austere anywhere else, but the yellow and red accents made it both chic and homey. From the sunflowers on her dining table to the red pillows on her sofa and bed, it just worked.

"If this place is any indication, you have excellent taste."

She thanked him. "It's a little much for some, but I

like it," she said. "Oh, would you like to see some of the designs I have in mind for the governor-elect's wife?"

He did. In fact, he wanted to hear all about her business.

Isaiah reluctantly released her from his embrace.

Sandra retrieved a tablet from her bag. She swiped her fingers across the screen a few times, before handing it to him.

As he scrolled through images of evening gowns, she picked up the television remote and turned up the volume. "I nearly forgot about the Howerton-Windom race," she said. "Did they say who won?"

"Janelle's dad is going to the state house of representatives," Isaiah said absently, absolutely riveted by Sandra's work.

"I'm happy for Mr. Howerton and Janelle." He heard her sigh in the background. "But Jordan put a lot of effort into trying to get Oliver Windom elected. He must be so disappointed."

"Politics is a rough game," Isaiah mumbled. His attention was focused on an image of an orange silk gown. He was no expert on women's clothing, but he knew enough to know what looked good, and the gowns he was gazing at were all stunning.

"I'll give him a call tomorrow," Sandra said.

Finally, Isaiah glanced up from the tablet. "Your designs are amazing," he said.

Sandra laughed. "You used to say the same thing back in high school."

"No, really," he said. "I don't think the governor-elect's wife will have a problem deciding on you as her designer. Her trouble will be picking one of these amazing gowns."

Sandra beamed up at him. "Thank you. Those words mean a lot coming from you."

It was true, Isaiah thought. "Your work really is amazing," he said. "I know I keep saying it, but it's the best word I can think of to describe it. *Amazing.*"

Sandra turned off the television and then switched off the lamp on the end table.

"I'm flattered you think the things I do with clothing are amazing." She slowly undid the top buttons on her blouse. "But I believe you'll find the things I can do out of my clothes *truly* amazing."

She slipped off the blouse, dangled it in one hand before letting it drop to the floor.

Isaiah licked his lips. His eyes were glued to her hand on the front clasp of her black lace bra, and his cock was hard as a rock.

Sandra pivoted and began to walk slowly down the hallway toward her bedroom. Removing her bra, she flung it over her shoulder.

Isaiah caught it with one hand as he followed her, prepared to be amazed.

Chapter 11

A week later, Sandra pulled a nearly completed gown from a cloth garment bag for her client's final fitting.

"Oh, my! It's exquisite." Octavia Hall gasped. She covered her mouth with her hand at the sight of it, and then her red lips firmed into a hard line. "This will help me show that bastard I'm married to, and his barely legal girlfriend."

Sandra smiled, gratified her client was pleased.

A Swoon Couture gown usually took months to go from imagination to finished product. However, in light of Octavia having been one of her first customers, whose influence had helped build her fledgling business, Sandra had accelerated the process. She'd quickly made a pattern for the design her client had selected, and pulled two of the three seamstresses she contracted off other gowns to work exclusively on this one.

Despite the frantic rush, the dress was indeed exceptional, and perfect for Octavia, Sandra thought. The garment's bodice was satin, in a shade of metallic copper that would pick up the golden tones of the older woman's skin, while the floor-length skirt was fashioned in a blush-pink swath of flowing silk.

She could hardly wait to see her client in it.

Octavia quickly shed her cashmere sweater and wool slacks, and Sandra helped her into the dress.

This time the gasp came from Sandra. "Y-you look beautiful," she stammered.

The word *beautiful* was an understatement. Octavia had always been a striking woman and was aging exceptionally well. However, the sight of her in the gown caught even Sandra by surprise.

Crossing the fitting room to retrieve a wrist pin cushion from the cabinet, Sandra returned to find her client staring at herself in the three-way mirror. Sandra went through her normal paces for fittings, and began studying the dress from every angle, looking for spots requiring mirror alterations. She paused when she noticed Octavia hadn't moved. Her client continued to stare at her reflection, frozen to the spot.

"Are you okay?" Sandra asked. "You need me to get you a bottle of water or something?"

"I'm fine, dear." The older women nodded absently, but her gaze remained fixed on her reflection. "It's just this dress. I haven't seen myself look like this in quite a long time."

Sandra could see tears forming in Octavia's eyes, but the woman quickly blinked them back.

"It's the perfect dress for you," Sandra said, and then

the description she'd been searching for popped into her head. "You look like royalty."

Her heartfelt words sounded corny aloud, until Octavia agreed with her assessment. "I do look regal, don't I? Like a queen."

She did.

Sandra's chest could barely contain the swell of emotion. This was the part of her business her father didn't see. Even if he did, he'd never understand it.

At heart, Swoon Couture wasn't about fashion or pretty dresses, she thought. It was about how those dresses, which started out as fuzzy images on the edge of her imagination, made women feel.

Sandra glanced at Octavia's reflection in the mirror, detecting a shift in the woman's demeanor. Octavia's spine seemed to stiffen as she pulled her shoulders back and lifted her chin.

However, the biggest change was in her face. The hard line of her mouth softened as she smiled, making her appear younger than her years. "I can't continue to let his behavior eat away at me," she said. "I'm better than bitter and worthy of more than revenge."

Octavia Hall had always been a client, not a friend, but hearing her revelation, Sandra couldn't stop herself from wrapping the older woman in a brief, sisterly hug.

"I can't explain it, but seeing myself in this dress…" Octavia paused and dabbed at the corners of her teary eyes with a fingertip. "It gave me back something I think I lost in the midst of the hurt and anger. My *pride*."

Sandra sniffed back a tear of her own. "I don't think I've ever been more proud of anyone."

Octavia acknowledged the sentiment with a single nod. "Now, let's get on with this fitting," she said. "I need to instruct my attorney to stop stalling and give my husband his quickie divorce. It's time for me to let go."

Soon Sandra was kneeling, marking the hem at the bottom of the gown, while her client chattered about the latest happenings in Wintersage. The gossip featured women who were also customers, so she restricted her response to an occasional and noncommittal *hmm*.

"Oh, I was surprised to hear you and the Jacobs boy were back together again," Octavia said matter-of-factly.

Sandra gulped, nearly swallowing the straight pin between her lips.

"He's barely home from his navy stint, and you've already snatched him up," her client went on, oblivious to Sandra nearly choking. "Can't say I blame you, as he certainly is easy on the eye. *Extremely* easy."

Rising to her feet, Sandra pulled the pin from her mouth. "You're mistaken," she said. "Isaiah Jacobs is in town, but we're not together."

Since the night of the Halloween party, she and Isaiah had been careful. They hadn't wanted their parents or anyone else to see them together and get the wrong idea about their relationship. Except for early-morning walks on the beach, they hadn't been anywhere together publicly in Wintersage.

The two of them had continued the nightly cooking sessions, of course, in preparation for the big Thanksgiving showdown. They'd also continued their sessions between the sheets, but Sandra knew her bedroom walls weren't talking.

"Are you sure about that?" Octavia raised a well-groomed eyebrow.

No way she could know about them, Sandra thought. Like Vicki, her client had simply heard about her and

Isaiah's brief chat at the Halloween party, and jumped to conclusions.

It was time to set her straight, before this went any further.

"I'm positive." Sandra matched that raised brow with one of her own.

The knowing smile on Octavia's face said she wasn't buying it. "That's strange," she said easily, then named another of Sandra's clients, one of Wintersage's most notorious gossips. "According to her, the two of you looked very much *together* at an art exhibit in Boston."

The Modern Furniture as Art exhibit at the Museum of Fine Arts she'd accompanied Isaiah to last weekend.

Damn, Sandra thought. Her mom was crazy about Isaiah. If she got wind of this, she'd be on the phone with Janelle trying to plan a wedding, a wedding that would never take place.

Sandra exhaled and decided the best tactic would be to enlist her client's help in squashing the rumors before they reached Isaiah's folks, or even worse, Nancy Woolcott.

She briefly explained that she and Isaiah were simply friends taking in an art exhibit. "That's all there is to it," Sandra said. "So I'd really appreciate you using your influence to put an end to any misleading gossip."

Octavia shrugged. "I'll do what I can, dear, but I expect it'll be difficult to contradict what people have seen with their own eyes."

"I don't understand," Sandra said.

The entire town couldn't have seen them at the exhibit, and she knew Janelle and Vicki wouldn't betray her confidence.

"She snapped a picture of one of the pieces on display, and managed to capture the two of you holding hands in the background. It's on her Facebook page," Octavia said.

"Damn." This time Sandra muttered the word aloud.

Octavia placed a gentle hand on her shoulder. "Unfortunately, in this day and age, a cell phone camera and social media are a nosy town's best friends."

Isaiah sat behind his father's desk at the headquarters of Martine's Fine Furnishings, examining the company's profit and loss statements, but not finding the answer to his question in the numbers.

Why?

Despite his wealthy roots, Isaiah had supported himself all his adult life. So he wasn't oblivious to the recession. However, as the economy recovered in the New England area, profits at Martine's had remained stagnant, and the company had laid off nearly fifty workers over the past two years.

His parents, due back from Orlando at the end of the week, had called the company's dwindling earnings simply a rough patch. Martine's cash position was healthy enough to withstand it. Still, an answer to Isaiah's question both plagued and evaded him.

Why?

He pushed back from the heavy oak desk that had once belonged to his mother's grandfather, and rose from the leather executive chair. One thing was for sure—he wasn't going to find out what he wanted to know sitting in this ivory tower. It was time to put boots on the ground.

He picked up the phone and punched in the extension for the warehouse. "Is Anthony Green working today?"

Moments later, Tony came on the line.

"Have the assistant supervisor take over your shift, and meet me in my father's office," Isaiah said. "I need your help."

Isaiah grabbed his overcoat. Bypassing the elevator, he took the stairs down the three flights to the first floor. He met his old teammate crossing the lobby.

"I'd heard you were working out of your parents' offices, but after what you said a few weeks ago I wasn't sure what to believe," Tony said.

"Take a ride with me up to Nashua." Isaiah named the location of Martine's largest store, just across the New Hampshire border. "I'll tell you all about it."

As the two walked to the spot reserved for his parents' cars in the company lot, Tony stopped in his tracks. He frowned at Isaiah's truck.

"I thought I was imagining things the first time I saw you in it, but this is the same beater we rode around in back in high school," he said. "Don't your folks have a spare BMW or Benz sitting in their garage?"

"I prefer mine." Isaiah opened the driver's side door. He'd sold the small car, which he'd almost had to fold himself in two to drive, before he'd left Italy. Since he was home for only a few weeks, there was no real reason for him to purchase a new vehicle.

Besides, he'd missed his old truck.

Tony settled into the passenger seat and pulled the seat belt over his protruding gut. "Folks are going to think I hitched a ride with a hillbilly," he grumbled.

Isaiah threw his head back and laughed, remembering his father uttering the same words on their trips to the radiation center.

"So what's the deal with Martine's?" Tony asked.

"First you say you aren't taking it over, but you're in your parents' offices and they're nowhere around. Then there's the rumor circulating about your folks selling."

Isaiah accelerated on the entrance ramp leading to the highway. "It's not a rumor. They are selling the business."

Tony whistled through his teeth. "I knew business has been down, but I didn't see that coming," he said. "Your folks sleep, eat and breathe Martine's."

"That's exactly why they decided to sell." Isaiah explained that his parents were looking forward to spending time together and enjoying the fruits of their labor after years of devotion to the company.

"What does this mean for my job?"

"I wish I had a better answer for you, but I honestly don't know," Isaiah said. "There were layoffs even before they decided to sell. I'm sure my folks will do their best to help their present employees keep their positions, but they can't predict or control what a new buyer will do."

He switched lanes and caught his old classmate's shrug in his peripheral vision.

"So what are we doing now?" Tony asked.

"Satisfying my curiosity," Isaiah said. "I've been over the books, and I'm having a hard time figuring out how come sales are still soft in spite of the economy improving."

Martine's was still making money, but the profit margin was getting slimmer every quarter.

"We're delivering regularly to the more affluent towns, but it's gradually slowed in middle- and working-class areas," Tony said.

Isaiah nodded. "I want to visit a few of the stores this

week, starting with Nashua and Merrimack, and see if I can get a feel for what's going on," he said. "You've worked at Martine's for nine years, so you'll have insight into things I might miss. Besides, I trust you and your judgment."

"I'm not sure what you're looking for, but I'll do whatever I can to help."

Located just across the state line and near the Pheasant Lane Mall shopping center, their first stop was one of the company's most profitable stores, because of New Hampshire's lack of sales tax. However, even its once robust sales were slipping.

They were greeted by a friendly salesman moments after walking in. Isaiah told the man they were just browsing, and he gave them their space, but let them know he was nearby if needed.

As they browsed the showroom, they were approached periodically by unobtrusive salespeople offering them a drink or to answer any questions.

"The service doesn't appear to be a problem," Isaiah said, more to himself than to Tony. Then again, the place didn't seem to have many customers.

He'd initially expected that inattentive service might be turning off potential customers. That certainly didn't appear to be the case here, and the staff had no idea of his family ties to the company.

Isaiah walked around the showroom, taking in the heavy, ornate furniture. They were well-made, quality pieces, but while some of the same furniture graced his parents' large house, it was hard for him to picture it in an average home. Most of it looked more suited for a museum display than actual use.

He sat on one of the sofas of a living room set. Frowning, he turned over the price tag.

Pushing himself off the hard upholstered cushion, he walked over to Tony, who was looking at a bedroom set.

"You see many orders for this one at the warehouse?" Isaiah asked.

"Not really."

"I'm not surprised. It looks like it belongs in a nineteenth-century English manor."

Tony scanned the huge matching pieces. "Also, I don't think most folks have a master bedroom big enough to accommodate the entire set."

"You get a generous employee discount. You have any Martine's furniture in your house?"

His old classmate looked down at his shoes.

Isaiah sighed. "Come on, man. I'm asking you as a friend."

Tony shook his head. "The wife doesn't like it. She thinks it looks like the stuff in her grandma's house."

As if on cue, the bell over the front door chimed and a white-haired couple walked in. A salesman accompanied them to the dining room sets.

"I see your wife's point." Isaiah thought of Sandra's bright, contemporary furnishings and couldn't help comparing them to the pieces his family's firm sold.

Martine's furniture was beautifully crafted, but it was too heavy, too ornate, too big and too impractical for the average customer. He revealed his family ties to the staff and spoke with a few of them. The conversations gave him an idea of what they were up against trying to sell the stuff.

One of the store's top salespeople summed it up. "Most of the newlyweds and new home owners walk in, take one look at our furniture and walk right back out the door."

Isaiah drove north to the Merrimack store, where he and Tony encountered a nearly identical scenario.

"Find what you were looking for?" his friend asked on the drive back to Wintersage.

Isaiah nodded. "But I get the feeling all I had to do was ask you in the first place."

"Don't get me wrong, your folks are good people to work for and they've been fair with me," Tony said. "However, my opinion is rarely sought out on anything but stock and deliveries."

If Isaiah were running Martine's that would be one of his first changes. He'd also clean house at the company's design department and start from scratch with fresh talent and new ideas.

However, it was a moot point. He was there just a few more weeks, and he'd only wanted to figure out what was going on with the company's dwindling bottom line. Mission accomplished. He'd tell his parents what he'd found out, and they could do whatever they saw fit with the information.

Isaiah braked at the tollbooth at the southbound entrance to the turnpike and paid the fare.

"So I take it you're still planning to leave Wintersage in a few weeks?" Tony asked.

Isaiah nodded. "The day after Thanksgiving."

"Does that mean Sandra is leaving with you?"

The truck swerved slightly as Isaiah did a double take. Where in hell had that come from? With the exception of her girlfriends, no one knew about him and Sandra.

"No," he answered truthfully. "But why do you ask?"

Tony shrugged. "I dunno," he said. "I saw a pic of you two together on one of the social-media sites..."

"Whoa," Isaiah said, knowing his friend had to be mistaken. They hadn't been anywhere together in Wintersage, and they definitely hadn't posed for a photo. "I'm not sure who was in the picture you saw, but it definitely wasn't me and Sandra."

"Well, it certainly looked like you two."

Isaiah faced the road in front of him, not wanting the smile on his face, which he had every time he as much as thought about Sandra, to give him away. "Then it couldn't have been recent," he said confidently.

Tony dug into his coat pocket and retrieved his phone. He swiped at the face of it and then held it up.

Isaiah glanced at the screen.

It was them, all right. They were indeed holding hands, and from his expression, it looked as if he couldn't wait to get Sandra back home and to bed.

Again, Isaiah had to silently admonish himself. It wasn't his home or his bed, even though he'd slept beside her nearly every night since they'd laid eyes on each other on Halloween. The arrangement hadn't been planned or even discussed between them; it came into being because they both wanted it night after glorious night.

"So are you going to continue to deny it?" Tony asked.

Screw it, Isaiah thought. While neither of them had wanted their families jumping to the wrong conclusion and mistaking their relationship for a long-term commitment, he and Sandra were both adults. Whatever they did or didn't do was nobody's business but theirs.

"We're just old friends," Isaiah said.

He caught Tony's raised brow out the corner of his eye. "Sandra Woolcott is fine as hell," his old classmate said. "You gonna be able to say goodbye to that in two weeks?"

Isaiah nodded. It wouldn't be easy to leave her again, but he would.

However, he didn't want to think about leaving now.

All he wanted to do was get back to Wintersage, because tonight he and Sandra were making sweet potato casserole.

Chapter 12

"Are you sure about this?"

Sandra heard Isaiah ask the question from the bedroom as she checked her appearance in her bathroom mirror. She plucked a bobby pin from the vanity and stuck it in her hair to anchor her updo.

"Not really, considering it's the last Saturday before Thanksgiving, and I need another practice run on the turkey." She shook her head at her reflection, remembering their last burned-on-the-outside, frozen-on-the-inside culinary effort. "But Janelle's one of my best friends, and I need to at least put in an appearance at her father's victory party. We won't stay long."

"You talk to your brother?"

Sandra pulled a red lipstick from her makeup bag. "Jordan was invited, but he's not coming. Says he's been preoccupied with the campaign for months and needs to spend time with his son."

"That's probably for the best," Isaiah said. "Is he still considering contesting the election results?"

Sandra spritzed her favorite perfume on the pulse point at her neck. "He's already filed the petition. He's waiting for it to be certified by the commonwealth's election division. I expect that bomb to drop any day now." She pivoted in the mirror to make sure her form-fitting, backless, red lace dress was on point. "Meanwhile, I'm going to enjoy a pleasant evening at the party Janelle worked hard planning for her dad."

Emerging from the bathroom, Sandra froze at the sight of Isaiah dressed in a dark suit and pristine white shirt. He'd eschewed the formality of a tie, and the open top buttons of his shirt revealed a hint of the broad chest she used as a pillow every night.

The man looked good enough to eat, and Sandra could hardly wait to get him back here for another taste.

"Wow." His eyes rounded. "I'm sure you think it's just a line I use to get into those lace panties of yours, but I've really never seen a woman more beautiful than you."

Already in her stilettos, Sandra didn't have to stretch far to plant a kiss on his lips. "By now you should know you don't need a line." She wiped the red lipstick print off his mouth with her thumb. "One look from you melts the panties right off me."

Isaiah inclined his head toward the bed they'd reluctantly abandoned to get ready. "Are you absolutely sure we need to show our faces at this party?"

Sandra followed his gaze. "We won't stay long," she said. "And since everyone thinks we're together now anyway, there's no use going through the pretense of showing up separately."

He exhaled. "I know. My folks have been on my

case, ever since they got back from their weekender in Myrtle Beach, to have you over to the house."

"Tell me about it. My dad is hoping Dale Mills will miraculously grow on me, but my mother has been grilling me about our nonrelationship since she saw the photo of us together at the museum."

Sandra laughed as they simultaneously repeated her client's statement, and now their favorite inside joke. "A cell phone camera and social media are a nosy town's best friends."

By the time they arrived, Darren Howerton's victory party was in full swing. Sandra had been on the Howerton estate hundreds of times since childhood, but she'd never seen it look more festive than it did tonight.

Red and blue balloons along with silver streamers bobbed against the high ceilings of the stately home while a live band played an up-tempo tune in the background. Sandra looked at the flag-inspired bunting over the windows and the Howerton campaign posters scattered artfully throughout. She saw the word *WINNER* had been stamped on the posters in large black letters, and was glad her brother had decided to stay home.

Jordan was still wrestling with his disappointment. Also, he wasn't convinced Janelle's father was the fair-and-square winner of the election.

She felt Isaiah's large palm on the bare skin of her back and warm tingles radiated throughout her body. "You okay?" he whispered against her ear.

Sandra nodded as she spotted Vicki and Janelle headed in their direction. Vicki's hair was swept up in its usual chignon, and she wore a raw silk sheath in a universally flattering shade of midnight blue. Pearls adorned her ears and neck.

As they approached, Sandra didn't notice anything about Janelle beyond the blissful smile she'd worn ever since she'd become Mrs. Ballard Dubois last month. One look at her, and a woman would think marriage was the best beauty treatment ever.

"So you two finally decided to stop sneaking around and be seen together in public?" Janelle asked.

"We're just—" Sandra began.

"Friends," Janelle and Vicki said in unison.

"You've both certainly told us enough times," Janelle added, referring to the occasions they'd seen Isaiah over the past two weeks, when he'd stopped by the Victorian to walk her home after work.

"And we're not buying it." Vicki's gaze dropped to their joined hands.

It had seemed so natural that Sandra hadn't even realized she and Isaiah were holding hands. A lot of things were happening between them naturally.

Isaiah cleared his throat. "I don't remember hearing about either of you getting back to Sandra on our dinner invitation," he said. "We've got another practice run before she has to cook Thanksgiving dinner solo on Thursday, and could use some turkey tasters."

Sandra pressed her lips together to keep from laughing aloud at the comical expressions on her friends' faces.

"How about it, ladies?" Isaiah asked.

Janelle looked at her watch. "Ballard's been in my father's study on a business call for nearly an hour," she said. "I'd better go find my husband before he misses the entire party."

Sandra watched as her friend practically sprinted in her high heels to get away from them.

"That leaves just you, Vic," Isaiah said. "Can we pencil you in for dinner tomorrow?"

"Um...I think I hear my parents calling me," she said. "They're here tonight, along with everyone else's."

Sandra groaned aloud, along with Isaiah, as Vicki made an exit as quickly as Janelle had moments earlier.

"So whose folks do we go in and greet first, yours or mine?" Sandra asked, gearing herself up for the task.

"Neither," Isaiah said, as they walked toward the sounds of music and conversations coming from the Howertons' conservatory. "First, we're going to congratulate Janelle's dad, and then I want to dance with you at least once before we go stirring up that hornets' nest."

There was a line of well-wishers waiting to speak with Darren Howerton, so they decided to hold off until after their dance. En route to the dance floor, Sandra caught sight of an especially elegant-looking Octavia Hall across the room. She was wearing a velvet cocktail dress in a sumptuous shade of forest green and was deep in conversation with a tall, distinguished man Sandra had never seen before.

Isaiah pulled her into his arms, and Sandra closed her eyes briefly and inhaled his clean, masculine scent. *Friends*, she reminded herself, just as they'd had to constantly remind everyone else. Still, she didn't want to think about Thanksgiving being a few short days away, and the fact that he was leaving the day after.

She peered over his shoulder. Once again her gaze landed on her client, just as the handsome man Olivia was with leaned in and whispered something in her ear that made them both laugh.

Isaiah pulled Sandra closer. She sighed as his hand

caressed her bare back. Lord, she was going to miss him, she thought.

Swallowing the lump of emotion rising in her throat, she focused on Octavia. Only this time, Sandra noticed she wasn't the only one looking at the older woman.

Her soon-to-be ex-husband was staring longingly at his estranged wife, while a young woman—Sandra assumed she was his girlfriend—tugged at the sleeve of his suit coat, trying to get his attention.

Good luck with that, Sandra thought, studying the barely out-of-her-teens woman, who now appeared to be pouting. It seemed very much to Sandra as if Mr. Hall wanted his wife back.

"I'm thinking once we speak to Janelle's dad and say a quick hello to our folks, we can head for the exit." Isaiah's deep baritone rumbled through Sandra. "I don't want to drag you away from your friends, but we only have a few days together..." His voice trailed off.

She looked up at his handsome face. "I can't think of anything I'd like more."

A short while later they'd just finished congratulating Darren Howerton on his victory, and turned away to find themselves staring into the smiling faces of their mothers.

"How nice to see you two together again." Cecily gave Sandra's hand a quick squeeze.

The uncharacteristic gesture threw her. She hadn't seen Isaiah's mom in a couple months, but she nearly didn't recognize her.

The woman who was usually preoccupied with business calls during her dress fittings seemed relaxed. The firm, businesslike set to her jaw had softened, and she was actually smiling.

Isaiah clearly hadn't exaggerated the changes in her since his parents had decided to sell the furniture business.

"My daughter's been so tight-lipped, I had no idea they were a couple until I turned on my computer." Sandra's mom ignored the laser-beam side-eye she was shooting her way.

"But we're not—" Isaiah began.

"They certainly seem to have picked up where they left off ten years ago, haven't they?" Cecily cut off his protest and directed her question at Nancy.

An uneasy feeling crept over Sandra at the conspiring smiles on their mothers' faces. The two of them, former classmates at Wintersage Academy, had always been friendly, but now they were acting like best friends.

"Yes, they have," Nancy agreed. "I wouldn't be surprised if we were related by *marriage* soon."

"Mom." The word came out stronger than Sandra intended and sounded like the bark of a large dog. "Isaiah and I are good friends, but that's all."

"We're all good friends, dear," her mother said sweetly. A little too sweetly. "So I'm sure you won't mind that I've invited Isaiah's family to join us at your house for Thanksgiving dinner on Thursday."

Sandra felt her chin hit her chest as she stared openmouthed at her. "Please, Mom, tell me you didn't."

"Yes, she did, and I've already accepted the invitation," Isaiah's mother said.

"I'm not a very good cook, and my place is small," Sandra said, scrambling for an excuse.

"And you already ordered our Thanksgiving dinner, Mom," Isaiah said. "I had my mouth set for the faux turkey loaf you've been talking about, and you wanted something healthy for Dad."

Cecily waved him off with a fling of her hand. "A little bit of turkey won't hurt him, and it's the holiday."

Sandra never thought there would be a day she'd be looking forward to her father rescuing her from her mother, but she was relieved to see him walking toward them.

The smile on his face disappeared as he looked from her to Isaiah.

"Nice to see you again, Mr. Woolcott," Isaiah said.

Her father regarded him with a grunt and a curt nod, which earned him an elbow from his wife.

"I've invited the Jacobses to have Thanksgiving dinner with us at Sandra's," Nancy said.

"Why?" Stuart asked, making Sandra want to envelop him in a hug.

Her mother's lips firmed into a straight line as she glared at him. "Seeing as our children are so close, I thought it would be nice for us to all sit down to a nice family meal."

"Nice meal?" He frowned. "A longer line for the toilet is more like it."

"Stu!" Her mother's harsh whisper was loud enough for them all to hear.

"What?" Stuart asked. "All I did was tell the truth. The girl's a damned disaster in the kitchen."

Sandra rolled her eyes to the ceiling. She should have taken a cue from Jordan and just stayed home. Could this evening get any worse?

Then she heard Isaiah clear his throat. His face was hard, and his angry gaze was directed at her father.

And Sandra knew without a doubt this evening could and would get worse.

* * *

Isaiah wasn't the type of man who disrespected his elders, but he wasn't the kind of man who allowed his woman to be disrespected, either.

By anyone, not even her father.

She's not yours, he reminded himself, *not anymore.*

And it wasn't his fight.

Still, he noticed the nearly imperceptible slump of Sandra's shoulders in the face of Stuart Woolcott's criticism.

"Your daughter might have been distracted in the kitchen on previous occasions, but she is *not* a disaster," Isaiah said firmly.

Sandra's father crossed his arms over his chest. "You haven't had to pay a cleaning crew or get a visit from the fire department because she was, as you say, distracted," he countered.

Isaiah didn't want to argue, but there were some things that just flat out needed to be said.

"You're right," he conceded. "However, I've never seen anyone work as hard as Sandra has these past few weeks."

Stuart harrumphed in reply.

Isaiah saw Sandra gnawing at her lip. When they were in high school, she used to be able to tell exactly what was on his mind. He hoped she did now, and understood he would never insult her father. But he wouldn't kowtow to him, either.

Isaiah hoped his face conveyed what was in his heart. He hadn't been by her side these past years, but he'd always be *on her side*.

"Your daughter makes a mean stuffing. Her green beans are delicious, and her sweet potato casserole will melt in your mouth." His words were directed at Stuart, but his gaze remained on Sandra.

Isaiah was heartened to see her shoulders straighten. Her chin lifted off her chest. She graced him with one of her beautiful smiles and something deep down inside him shifted.

At that moment, he wanted nothing more than to wake up to her smile every morning for the rest of his life.

He blinked and quickly averted his eyes, banishing the errant thought back to the depths of his heart.

"Spoken like a man with his nose wide-open," Stuart said. "The navy might have given you a cast-iron stomach, but I'm bringing antacids, an antidiarrheal, a fire extinguisher and a take-out pizza menu to dinner on Thursday."

Isaiah's eyes narrowed. "Just don't forget the keys to your Chevelle. You'll want to have them handy when you're asking for seconds of Sandra's superb cooking."

Three pairs of Woolcott eyes rounded at his bold prediction, while his mother gave him a stern look.

The band continued to play in the background while the chatter of conversations went on around them.

A dry chuckle from Sandra's father finally broke the awkward silence. "Since my wife invited you all to dinner, there should be enough room at the table for one more guest."

"Who, dear?" his wife asked.

"I wouldn't want Dale Mills to miss out on our daughter's *superb* meal," he said.

"Good Lord." Sandra rolled her eyes. "Give it a rest, Dad."

A few weeks ago, he and Sandra would have shared

a laugh at the mention of Dale Mills. Now Isaiah found himself becoming annoyed at the possibility of her going out with him, or for that matter, any other man.

Stuart smiled at his daughter, before returning his attention to Isaiah. "You're still shipping out the day after Thanksgiving, right?" he asked.

"Yes, sir. That's always been the plan."

"Good," Stuart said. "With you gone, Sandra will be free and clear to hold up her end of the deal when she loses our little wager."

Chapter 13

Sandra paced her kitchen floor Tuesday evening, breaking her stride only to peek at the turkey inside her oven.

The bird she'd cooked on Sunday had been dry enough to pass for jerky, and with only two days left until Thanksgiving, tonight was her last practice run.

"Hovering won't make it cook any faster." Isaiah glanced up from the sketch pad he'd borrowed from her earlier. "Besides, I think we nailed it this time."

Sandra stopped midpace. She'd read and reread the recipe enough times to recite it from memory. Then Isaiah had read it aloud as she went through each step.

Still, she couldn't stop herself from peering through the oven window again.

"After the way you stuck up for me with my dad the other night, I don't want to let you or myself down."

Sandra picked up the spice jars on the counter to

double-check the labels. She didn't know Isaiah had abandoned the sketch pad until she felt his arms around her.

Sighing, she leaned back into his embrace. He took the small jar from her hand and returned it to the counter.

"You didn't mix anything up." He turned her around until she faced him. "And you could never let me down. Win or lose, I'm proud of you."

"Yeah, but if I lose, you're not stuck with Dale Mills for five agonizing dates."

Her tone had been jovial, but apparently Isaiah hadn't gotten the joke. His face turned to stone and his eyes darkened.

"You okay?" she asked, taken aback by the sudden change.

He opened his mouth as if about to say something, but instead only nodded.

"So how'd it go at The Quarterdeck last night?" He dropped his arms and, taking her hand, led her to the breakfast bar, where he'd been seated.

Sandra sat down beside him. She noticed he'd changed the subject from her potential dates with Dale, but wasn't sure what to make of it. She told him about her plan to meet Janelle and Vicki at the Victorian on Black Friday to go on a shopping spree in sales-tax-free New Hampshire.

"Janelle didn't bring up the recount, and I didn't, either. I love both Janelle and my brother, and won't let politics spoil either relationship."

Isaiah raised a brow. "Speaking of politics…?"

Sandra shook her head. "Still haven't heard a peep from the governor-elect's wife," she said. "I sent her my illustrations weeks ago. I thought for sure she would have made a decision on a designer by now."

She picked up the sketch pad he'd been doodling on. "Anyway, she said she'd let me know before Thanksgiving, and there's still tomorrow."

Isaiah leaned in and kissed Sandra. "That was for luck," he said. "However, I'm betting by Friday you'll have received good news from the governor-elect's wife, and be able to drive me to the airport in your newly won classic Chevelle."

Sandra forced a smile. She had no right to feel tightness in her chest at the thought of him leaving in a few days. After all, they'd made the terms of their nonrelationship clear before they'd taken things beyond a kiss. It was what Isaiah wanted. At the time, it was what she thought she'd wanted, too.

Turning the sketch pad over, Sandra tried to distract herself by looking at what he'd been drawing since she'd put the turkey in the oven.

"Furniture?" She scrunched up her nose in confusion.

Isaiah reached for the pad. "I was just messing around."

"No, I want to see." She pulled it out of his reach.

Ignoring his protests, Sandra studied the sleek, minimalist lines of the contemporary pieces. One was a black platform bed that looked plain at first glimpse, until she realized the headboard and night tables on either side were part of one large unit.

In an eye-catching twist, he'd drawn another bed anchored to the wall by the headboard, which made it appear as if it were floating.

"These designs are good, Isaiah, really good," she

said, flipping through more pages filled with illustrations of dining and living room pieces. "I'm impressed."

It was an understatement. Blown away was more like it.

Isaiah shrugged. "I'd never thought of furniture as an art form until we went to the museum exhibit in Boston. Some of the pieces were totally out there, but others were practical, sophisticated and quite beautiful," he said. "They were indeed art."

He frowned. "I wish the designers at Martine's could have seen that exhibit before it left," he said. "It might have inspired them, because the stuff they're doing now..." He shook his head.

"What do you think of this?" Sandra picked up the pencil and began sketching in details, building on his ideas with ones of her own.

She added lighting to the platform bed and a curve to the straight lines of the headboard. On a roll, she grabbed her colored pencils from her tote bag. With a few strokes, she shaded in the kidney-shaped, glass dining table he'd drawn in a blue that matched the color of the ocean outside their door.

Isaiah rose from his chair. She could feel his warm breath on her neck as she continued to make little tweaks here and there to his designs.

"Wow," he said.

"You like the additions?" she asked.

"Yeah, I do. I like them a lot. You have excellent taste, and a great eye. It was the first thing I picked up on when I walked into your house."

Sandra looked up from the sketch pad. She turned around in the chair and inclined her head toward the wall where they'd made love Halloween night. "It didn't seem like you were thinking about my taste or great eye the first time you walked in here."

He nuzzled her neck and ran his tongue over the pulse point he'd set to racing. "Oh, I was thinking about your taste, all right."

Sandra squirmed in her chair. She wanted to do a lot more, but the aroma of roasting turkey was filling the house and she could not screw up this bird.

She glanced at the oven timer. "Don't start something we can't finish for at least another half hour."

She went back to the sketchbook, and they continued to collaborate. Back in high school, he'd been focused on his painting, and she'd only cared about creating beautiful dresses. But this evening she discovered she liked them putting their heads together—the process as well as the results.

Sandra looked up at the strong, masculine face she'd grown accustomed to seeing every night before she fell asleep. "We work well together, don't we?" Her tone was soft and a bit sad as she allowed herself to dream of what might have been if they'd stayed together all those years ago.

"Perfectly," he replied.

"Then why, Isaiah?" The question came out before she could stop it. "Why didn't you stand up to your folks ten years ago? *Why didn't you stand up for us?*"

The oven timer chimed.

"You don't have to answer that." Sandra closed her eyes briefly. "I told you, I told myself, that I wouldn't ask those kinds of questions. Just enjoy the now."

Isaiah watched as she placed the sketchbook on the breakfast bar and slid off the chair. There were so many things he wanted to say to her, but his emotions were all over the place.

He couldn't pinpoint when it had occurred, but sometime between Halloween and tonight their fun and friendship had turned into something more. Feelings deeper and stronger than the ones they'd felt for each other in high school.

He'd fallen in love with Sandra Woolcott all over again.

She opened the oven door. Using pot holders, Isaiah lifted the heavy turkey from the oven and placed it on the stove.

"Well, at least it looks good." Sandra's voice was filled with faux cheerfulness that didn't reach her eyes.

He grasped her arms lightly and turned her until she faced him. "You deserve an answer to the question you asked me."

With a shake of her head, Sandra touched her fingers to his lips to stop him. "It was a long time ago. I should have never brought it up."

Isaiah kissed her fingertips, before pulling her hand away. "I handled things the way I did back then for the same reason we're doing what we're doing here." He gestured toward the perfectly browned turkey in the foil pan.

Sandra blinked. "I don't understand."

"I did it because I wanted to make my dad—a man who, despite his flaws, I love and respect—proud of me."

This time when Sandra blinked there were tears in her eyes. He cupped the side of her face and brushed one away with his thumb as he continued. "I was young and made the best decision I could at the time. Do I wish I'd handled it differently? Yes," he said. "Especially now that I've had a glimpse at the life I could have had."

Sandra stood on tiptoe and brushed her lips against his in the sweetest of kisses.

And Isaiah wondered if she instinctively knew how much he loved her.

Dinner that evening had been utter perfection. Sandra had to admit her turkey looked like it had been ripped from the pages of a glossy magazine.

However, neither of them had had much of an appetite.

"I think I'm just tired of turkey," Isaiah had offered in way of explanation.

Sandra had nodded in agreement as she'd pushed the food around her plate with her fork. Deep down, she knew the real reason for their lack of hunger.

In the few weeks they'd been together, Isaiah had made the same mistake as her.

He'd fallen in love.

There was no need for him to say it. Sandra saw it in his eyes. Heard it in his voice. Felt it in his touch. Isaiah loved her, all right, and she loved him, too.

But it changed absolutely nothing.

As the owner of Swoon Couture, Sandra lived her dream every day. She wouldn't destroy his by asking him to give up art school and stay in Wintersage. No matter how badly she wanted them to finally have a life together.

Awkward, polite small talk filled the rest of the evening, and a cloak of silence followed them to the bedroom.

Sandra sighed as she clung to her side of the bed,

forgoing what had become her nightly routine of falling asleep in Isaiah's arms.

She yearned for the naked man in her bed. Her body having grown accustomed to the heat of his kisses, the protectiveness of his strong embrace.

Sandra readjusted the pillow beneath her head. She longed to reach out to him, but dread stopped her.

All she could think about was the day after Thanksgiving when she'd have to say goodbye, and everything they'd shared these past few weeks would be a memory.

"You awake?" Isaiah's deep voice fill the darkened room illuminated by a sliver of moonlight streaming through the window shutters.

He smoothed a hand down the side of her bare hip, and she squeezed her eyes shut as if the gesture could stem the ripples of awareness his touch sent straight to her core.

"Yes," she whispered, unable to resist when he pulled her into his arms.

Sandra rested her chin on his broad chest and stared up at his face. She studied it in the moonlight, etching every plane and angle into her brain. His hardness pressed against her belly and moisture pooled at the juncture between her thighs.

Lifting her chin with his finger, Isaiah brushed his lips against hers. The gentle butterfly kiss belied the insistent throb of his erection.

He threaded his fingers through her hair and cradled her head in his hand. But instead of the deeper kiss she expected, he pinned her with his gaze.

"I came to your door Halloween night because I wanted you. More than I've ever wanted any other woman." Both his tone and gaze intensified. "Tonight,

I need you, Sandra. More than I've ever needed anyone in my life."

Sandra felt the barrier she'd futilely erected around
her heart shatter. His words touched a part of her soul
she hadn't known existed until now. They filled her
with an unabashed love that overwhelmed her trepida-
tion over their dwindling time together.

Isaiah crushed his mouth to hers, this kiss as hard
and insistent as his cock. Sandra kissed him back, refusing to allow the sadness awaiting her once he left
for London to keep her from enjoying the remaining
nights with this man.

For now, he was still her man.

It was Isaiah who finally broke off the kiss.

"Sandra, I lo—" he began, but she silenced him with
a shake of her head.

She didn't want to hear the words. They would only
make it more difficult when the time came for her to
let him go.

"Don't tell me," she said. *"Show me."*

Still holding her in his arms, Isaiah rolled over until
she was beneath him. Sandra gasped, relishing the
weight of his lean, muscular body pressing her into
the mattress.

Her fingers clung to his shoulders as she spread her
legs, and he united them with one smooth thrust.

"Isaiah," she cried out, arching her back to meet the
powerful stroke.

Rising to his elbows, his body stilled, and he stared
down at her. Sandra watched the moonlight dance over
his strong, masculine features revealing more than
words could convey.

Never had she felt more cherished. *So loved.*

Slowly, he began to move inside her. Their gazes remained locked as they found their rhythm. The playful sex that had been a hallmark of their friends-with-benefits relationship was absent tonight, replaced by something Sandra had never truly experienced until now, *lovemaking.*

Isaiah increased the pace, and she wrapped her legs around his waist as his strokes grew harder, deeper. Sandra ground her hips against his, unable to control her body's desperate, greedy response. The more he gave her, the more she wanted.

And she couldn't get enough of it. Of him.

As if he read her thoughts, Isaiah leaned in and nuzzled her neck, but his cock remained on task. Never missing a single pounding beat.

"How could I have ever believed I could get making love to you out of my system?" he rasped against the hollow of her throat.

Lost in the wonder of the magic their sweat-slicked bodies created, Sandra could only moan in response as she began to tremble beneath him. She was close. Oh, so close.

As in tune with her body as he was with her mind, Isaiah drove into her. His unrelenting pace rocked the big bed, sending the headboard crashing against the wall. Again and again.

"Isaiah!" Sandra screamed as the spasms of an orgasm overtook her.

He gripped her hips with his hands, pulling her even closer. Their escalating pants competed with the clamor of the headboard hitting the wall until moments later, when Isaiah exploded inside her.

The sound of her name and his declaration of love echoing in her ears.

Chapter 14

Sandra stared at the empty space in her bed. It was Thanksgiving morning. Isaiah had quietly slipped out a half hour or so ago, thinking she was asleep, but she'd lain awake most of the night, relishing the feel of his embrace for one of the last times.

Sandra skimmed her fingertips over the pillow that still bore his imprint. She couldn't think about how much she'd miss him. There would be plenty of time for that tomorrow, when he left for London.

Right now, she had to focus on their families showing up on her doorstep this afternoon. Some of them anticipating a holiday feast and others expecting a disaster.

Sandra exhaled and threw back the covers.

"Don't get up."

Sandra looked up to see Isaiah standing at the bedroom door bearing coffee and a familiar purple box with the bakery's logo. She'd been so absorbed in her thoughts she hadn't heard him return.

She inhaled the coffee, before taking a sip.

"I figured you could use a treat before our families descend on us today." He sat next to her on the bed and unearthed a cinnamon roll from the bag.

Sandra nodded her thanks. She bit into the cinnamon roll. As with all of Carrie's bakery treats, it was delicious, but this morning it didn't elicit Sandra's usual moans of delight.

All she could think about was tomorrow being their last morning together.

Stay.

Sandra swallowed the word on the tip of her tongue with another bite of the cinnamon roll.

"You didn't get one for yourself?" she asked, knowing Isaiah loved the bakery's cupcakes and cinnamon rolls almost as much as she did.

"I ate it on the way back here." The corner of his mouth tugged into a half smile that would have been a full-on laugh a few days ago. Before they'd both realized they were friends who had fallen in love.

Sandra polished off the roll, and then quickly showered and dressed in jeans and a sweater. Thanks to the decorations she and Isaiah had picked up earlier, and autumn floral arrangements from Vicki, her home had a warm and festive atmosphere.

She checked the dining table, which she'd set for nine last night, smoothing a hand over the orange tablecloth. She'd placed Vicki's stunning arrangements in the living room and created her own centerpiece using fresh green pears and amber votive candles, which she would light just before serving dinner.

"You ready to get started?" Isaiah pushed up the sleeves of his black sweater, and as always, she was immediately drawn to the corded muscle of his forearms. "What can I do?"

Sandra tied on her apron. "You can't help me. I have to cook every morsel with my own hands."

"I know, but nothing in the terms of your wager says I can't pull the ingredients from the fridge and cabinets or read the recipes aloud."

Sandra smiled up at his eager face, and Vicki's words came back to her yet again. *"A man who's truly your Prince Charming won't divert you from your goals. He'll want to be there to cheer you on..."*

Sandra closed her eyes briefly to pull herself together and get focused.

A beep sounded from her purse, which was hanging off the back of one of the kitchen chairs. Figuring it was a good-luck text from either Vicki or Janelle, she went to retrieve her phone, grateful for the distraction.

Sandra glanced at the missed-call alert on the screen, but it wasn't from her friends, after all.

"Everything okay?" Isaiah asked, after she finished listening to the message.

Stunned, Sandra looked up at him. "The governor-elect's wife called late last night." She grinned as the news from the phone call sank in. "She picked my gown to wear to the inaugural ball!"

Isaiah let out a whoop, picked Sandra up and spun her around. "I knew it. I just knew she'd pick yours," he said. "That orange silk gown was…"

"Amazing," Sandra finished.

They stared at each other a moment, before they both burst into laughter at the word he'd used initially to describe the gown, and then used repeatedly to describe the steamy sex they'd had that night.

It was their first light moment in two days, ever since they'd realized they were in love.

"She asked that I call her as soon as I got the message," Sandra said.

"On Thanksgiving?"

Sandra shrugged. "That's what she said."

Moments later, Sandra beamed as the governor-elect's wife praised her design.

"The other designers presented me with designs of black dresses that, frankly, all seemed to look alike," she said. "So when I saw yours—that gorgeous orange, and it's just my style—I *knew* it was the one."

The woman went on to apologize for not letting her know sooner. "I've simply been swamped since my husband was elected. It's turned our whole lives upside down, but in a good way."

Sandra thought she was about to end the call, but she continued, "I have a favor to ask of you. My husband and I have been invited to a state dinner at the White House. I'd like you to design a gown for me in one of the commonwealth's official colors, either blue or cranberry."

"The White House," Sandra gasped. Even better than the statewide exposure of the gown for the inaugural ball, this one would put Swoon Couture in the national, maybe even international, spotlight.

The governor-elect's wife laughed. "That was exactly my reaction when the First Lady called me yesterday afternoon."

"I'd be honored to design your gown."

"Well…" The woman on the other end of the line hesitated. "You haven't heard the rest of it yet."

Sandra's mouth dropped open as she heard the date of the state dinner. "B-but that's the weekend after next."

"Exactly, and since we're leaving the country early tomorrow morning for a few days, I'd need to see the design no later than this evening, which I know is a terrible imposition considering it's the holiday."

Sandra glanced up at Isaiah, who was pulling spices from the cupboards and arranging them on the black granite countertop. His iPod earbuds were crammed into his ears, and he bobbed his head in time with music only he could hear.

They'd both worked so hard to help her win this wager with her father. She knew all the recipes by heart, and the night before last she'd made the perfect turkey. The leftovers were in the refrigerator, next to the turkey she was to prepare for their families today.

Then she thought about her father. He'd never know that she could have pulled this dinner off. However, as his daughter, she possessed the same work ethic as Stuart Woolcott and knew what she had to do.

"I'll get to work on it right away," she said. "I'll email the proposed designs to you later today."

Ending the call, Sandra walked into the kitchen and touched a hand to Isaiah's shoulder. He pulled off the earbuds and smiled down at her. "So how'd it go?"

Sandra launched into a blow-by-blow of the conversation. She watched his face for signs of disappointment, but instead found understanding.

Then he broke out in a grin. "Do you have any idea how proud I am of you?"

His question surprised her.

"But I thought you'd be annoyed. All the trouble you went through." Then her mind raced ahead to contacting everyone to inform them—at the last minute on Thanksgiving—that dinner was canceled. "I'd better get busy calling our folks and Jordan to let them know dinner is off, so I can get to my studio."

Isaiah grasped her shoulders and kissed her soundly. "I'll handle everything with our families. You just get to work."

"They'll probably all be relieved."

Sandra quickly gathered her things. When she got to her front door, he was standing there holding out her coat for her, and she slipped her arms into the sleeves.

"Good luck," he said.

As she walked the short distance to the Victorian, Sandra knew Isaiah was indeed her Prince Charming.

But only for one more night.

Isaiah stared at the door he'd closed behind Sandra.

He'd left her with the impression that he was about to call their families to cancel Thanksgiving dinner and effectively call off Sandra's wager with her father.

But there were two things his training at Annapolis and years in the military had drilled into him: never give up and always have a backup plan.

Isaiah glanced at the clock on the fireplace mantel.

Now all he had to do was figure out what, exactly, was their plan B.

Chapter 15

It was late afternoon by the time Sandra had scanned and emailed a copy of her design sketch to the governor-elect's wife.

Despite the last-minute request, the dress had turned out even more beautiful than Sandra had expected. Designed of fluid chiffon in the requested color of cranberry, it featured a draped bodice and high slit that would accentuate the woman's sleek figure and compliment her sophisticated style.

Sandra inhaled the salty tang of the chilly November air as she walked back home, proud of her work.

But as her small house came into view, her quick steps came to an abrupt halt.

She blinked, hard.

"It can't be," she whispered aloud, taking in the familiar cars parked in front of her home. Her stomach dropped and she fought the urge to run in the opposite direction.

Isaiah was supposed to have contacted their families to let them know dinner was canceled. Why on earth were they here?

Sandra heard voices and football blaring from the television as she approached. Again she thought about jumping in her MINI Cooper and making a break for it.

"I don't see my daughter or any signs of dinner." Her father's voice came through the door. "Work or no work, we had a deal. So she'd better be figuring out where she'll be taking Dale to dinner next week."

Next came the deep rumble of Isaiah's baritone, but she couldn't make out what he'd said.

Sandra sighed and opened the door. She couldn't leave Isaiah on his own to deal with them, even if he deserved it for not phoning them to cancel.

"Happy Thanksgiving, everyone," she called out brightly, trying to put a happy spin on what was surely going to be a miserable evening.

"Bye!" Mason shouted, and he ran toward her like a miniature tornado.

Sandra knelt and caught her nephew in her arms. She smothered his little face in kisses before setting his squirming body on his feet.

She looked up to see Isaiah standing in front of her. He helped with her coat. Before she could ask what was going on, he looked down at her with his intense dark gaze and silently mouthed two words.

Trust me.

And although she had no idea where he was going with this, she put her faith in him.

Sandra walked into her living room with Isaiah by

her side. Her brother and dad were sitting on the sofa watching football, while Isaiah's father watched the game from an armchair.

Stuart looked pointedly at the clock on the mantel. "So you finally decided to show your face," he said.

"I had to work, Dad."

"So your *friend* here told us." He inclined his head toward Isaiah.

"I was designing a dress for the governor-elect's wife to wear to a state dinner at the White House."

"That's wonderful, dear." Her mother came in from the dining room, and Cecily followed.

"Congratulations. That's quite an accomplishment," Isaiah's mother chimed in. She looked at her husband, who was totally engrossed in the football game. "Isn't it, Ben?"

"Happy Thanksgiving," Ben said absently, his eyes still glued to the television.

Sandra thanked the two women and then turned to her father. Surely a workaholic like him could appreciate her situation.

She held her breath, as he looked her up and down. "I don't see a bucket of chicken in your arms," he said. "So where's this melt-in-your mouth meal Jacobs here was going on about the other night at the party?"

Clearing his throat, Jordan rose from the sofa and joined them. "Happy Thanksgiving, Sandra." Her brother leaned in as if he was about to hug her, but instead whispered in her ear. "If you manage to shut Dad up by somehow winning this bet, I think I'll give you my car, too."

He winked, and Sandra smiled up at him, grateful to have his support.

A commercial came on the television, interrupting the game, and Isaiah's father finally broke away from the screen. He got up from his chair and kissed her on the cheek.

"I was preoccupied with the game earlier, but it's always lovely to see you, Sandra," Ben said. "And it's especially nice seeing you and my son together."

A grunt sounded from her father's direction. "Dale is having dinner with his family today." He directed his words at Sandra. "However, I mentioned you and I might stop over later for dessert. If that cold stove in your kitchen is any indication, you're going to have something to ask him."

Nancy frowned and shook her head at her husband. "Oh, Stu," she said in an admonishing tone, before turning to Sandra. "But we're all starting to get hungry."

Isaiah's father nodded in agreement. "As much as I'd like to be the one to give Stuart a ride home after he loses that Chevelle, it's not looking real good for you, Sandra," he said. "I'm hungry, too, and it doesn't smell like Thanksgiving around here."

Grumbles about dinner sounded from everyone, except Jordan, who had taken a drowsy Mason into the spare bedroom for a nap. Sandra didn't know what Isaiah had been thinking by not calling them to cancel. Both sets of parents were enough to deal with on a regular day, even worse when they were crabby from hunger.

"Just hold on, everyone!" Isaiah's deep voice echoed through the living room, silencing their complaints. "Sandra just walked through the door after putting in a full day at work. If you could just wait—"

Ben cut him off, mumbling something about locating a pizza delivery menu.

"If you can't hear me out, Dad, you can always go home and enjoy that tasty faux turkey loaf from the meal delivery service." Isaiah turned to his mother. "Right, Mom?"

"Definitely. They brought our white bean turkey to the house this morning." Cecily raised her hands and made air quotes around the word *turkey*. "In fact, why don't I just pop home and get it? There's plenty for all of us."

Sandra watched as both Isaiah and his father made faces that would have been hilarious if she didn't practically have a Thanksgiving mutiny on her hands.

"Um…let's just hear what Isaiah has to say," Ben suggested.

"Why don't you all just have a seat in the living room and enjoy the game," Isaiah said. "Dinner will be served in about a half hour."

A half hour. Sandra's eyes rounded. How on earth was she going to get dinner on the table in thirty minutes with a raw turkey in her refrigerator?

Isaiah took her by the hand. "Let's get started, sweetheart."

Her father rose from the sofa and followed them into the kitchen. "Oh, no. You can't help her cook." Stuart wagged a finger in his direction. "The terms of our wager are very specific."

Isaiah grinned at her dad, and Sandra silently pleaded with him to stop goading him. Isaiah would be long gone tomorrow, and she'd be the one stuck listening to the incessant gloating once she lost the bet.

"I have no intention of cooking. I'll simply be sitting at the breakfast bar offering your daughter some moral support."

"That had better be all you do, Jacobs." Her father grunted.

"You'll also adhere to the exact terms of the bet, correct?" Isaiah asked.

"Of course," Stuart replied. "And just to remind you, with my girlfriend on the line, I'm expecting turkey, green beans, sweet potatoes—"

"And something with apples," Isaiah finished.

"Exactly." Her father pointed at his eyes with two fingers, and then pointed one at Isaiah. "I'll only have one eye on the game. I'm keeping the other one on you."

Sandra tied on her apron as her father retreated to a chair in the living room that gave him a better view of the kitchen. She opened her refrigerator, but didn't spot a miracle inside it, only the uncooked turkey and the leftover one from the other night.

She closed the door and looked up at Isaiah expectantly. "What now?" she asked.

He picked up the cookbook they'd been using, opened it and pointed to a recipe she hadn't seen before.

Sandra quickly skimmed it and beamed up at him.

He returned her smile with a huge grin. "It's time to unleash plan B."

Sandra stood at the breakfast bar, hands on her hips, studying the recipe.

This just might work out, after all, she thought, if she didn't screw it all up with one of her kitchen mishaps.

She glanced up at Isaiah again.

He silently mouthed the word *focus*.

Isaiah had always maintained she'd never had a cooking problem, only a problem staying focused while she was in the kitchen.

Sandra closed her eyes and blocked everything from her mind except the recipe. Exhaling, she opened them, preheated the oven and quickly began assembling the ingredients, including the leftover turkey from the other night she'd cooked to perfection.

They'd eaten the turkey's legs. However, the breast was still intact.

She got busy dicing it into small chunks as she waited for her saucepan of chicken broth on the stove to boil. Then she started chopping baguettes into one-inch pieces.

"She should stop wasting everyone's time and just give up." Sandra heard her father in the other room. "Anybody know if the Chinese restaurant is open today? Do they deliver?"

"Stu!" her mother admonished, in a whisper loud enough for everyone to hear.

"Focus," Sandra muttered to herself, as she glanced at the recipe book again. She looked up to find Isaiah nodding in agreement, and could feel the encouragement radiating from his intense dark gaze.

She moved through the next steps of the recipe, adding sweet potatoes and green beans to the boiling broth to cook for only the minutes it took for her to dice apples and a large onion.

Sandra swiped at her brow with the back of her arm. She drained the potatoes and green beans, as butter melted in a large skillet.

After dicing the sweet potatoes and green beans, she finally added all the ingredients to the skillet, along with chopped fresh sage. She double- and triple-checked the spices, sprinkled them over the mixture and pulled the carton of eggs from the refrigerator.

Ten minutes later, she dished the contents of the skillet onto eight plates and topped them with sunny-side-up eggs. She took the warm plates to the dining room two at a time, while Isaiah pulled out bottles of chilled wine and called everyone to the table. She was lighting the candles when they'd finally all gathered.

Her father looked down at his plate as he sat down at the table. "What's this supposed to be?" A frown creased his face.

"It's Sandra's Thanksgiving Hash," she proclaimed.

Mason, who was seated in a plastic booster seat in a chair next to his father, immediately grabbed a fistful of food off his plate and jammed it into his mouth. "Good," he yelled, bobbing his little head.

The move incited a wave of laughter around the entire table.

Jordan smiled at his son. "Mason here just added a new word to his vocabulary," he said. "So if my boy says it's good, that should be enough of a recommendation for all of us to try it."

"Well, it certainly smells like Thanksgiving," Ben said.

"I agree," Cecily chimed in. "It looks delicious, Sandra."

Sandra wanted to spring from the table and hug both her nephew and Isaiah's parents. Ben and Cecily were right; the hash looked and smelled great.

"First we need to say grace," Nancy said. "Stu, Ben, either of you want to do the honors?"

After a suggestion from Ben to keep it short, Stuart said a quick blessing. Sandra held her breath as she looked around the table for their reactions after their first bites.

Nothing.

Not a peep. All she heard was the sound of cutlery scraping against plates. She looked at Isaiah, who was seated at the other side of the table. He inclined his head toward his plate and nodded his seal of approval.

Now that she'd gotten through cooking with no mishaps, Sandra dug into her own plate. Her nephew had been right. *It was good.*

As the eating began to wind down, Isaiah's father was the first to comment. "While I admit this wasn't exactly what I was expecting for Thanksgiving, it was excellent, Sandra." He glanced at his empty plate. "I think I inhaled it."

From the looks of the other empty plates, they all had, she thought. Sandra gazed at her father expectantly.

"Ben's right. I'll concede that the food was edible, and there were no disasters in its preparation," he said.

Sandra sighed. It was as close to a compliment as she'd get from him, so she'd take it.

"Edible?" Her mother's voice was incredulous. "Stuart Woolcott, you cleaned your plate and then polished off the rest of mine."

Jordan chimed in. "I think I saw him lick his fingers."

"I—I did not." Her dad looked down at his hands as if checking to make sure.

"Good! Good! Good!" Mason chanted his new word and banged his small fist on the table.

Jordan patted him on the head. "Mason's absolutely right," he said. "Dad, don't you think there's something you should be handing over to Sandra?"

"What?" Their father picked up his wineglass.

Nancy narrowed her eyes. "The car keys, Stu."

"H-huh?" Stuart sputtered. "Okay, maybe she didn't screw it up, and maybe her cooking was just as melt-in-your-mouth as Jacobs here said." He gestured toward Isaiah. "But the terms of our wager were specific, and Sandra's Thanksgiving Hash was *not* on the menu we agreed on."

"I beg to differ, sir." Isaiah spoke for the first time since they'd sat down to eat. "You asked for turkey, stuffing, green beans, sweet potatoes and something with apples, correct?"

"I did, but she knew what I meant!" Stuart said.

"It's not about what you meant," Isaiah replied. "It's about the exact terms of the bet."

"Isaiah's right, Dad," Jordan stated.

Sandra saw sweat break out on her father's forehead as Isaiah's dad rubbed his hands together and, ignoring his wife's censoring stare, laughed manically.

"Admit it, Stu," Nancy said. "Sandra outsmarted you and won your bet fair and square."

Thanks to Isaiah. Sandra looked across the table at him. The victory was almost at hand, but all she felt was heartache. How in the world would she be able to say goodbye to him tomorrow?

"But it's not fair. I wasn't expecting—" her father began, but her mother cut him off midsentence.

"Sandra's a Woolcott, which makes her the proverbial chip off the old block. You underestimated her," Nancy said. "Now it's time to pay the price."

Stuart nodded once at his wife, stood and reached into his pants pocket. He pulled out his key ring, took off the keys to his beloved 1970 Chevelle SS and handed them to Sandra.

"Thank you, Dad," she said.

Her father shrugged. "Everyone's right. You won our bet fair and square. Congratulations."

Sandra looked into her father's eyes. She'd always seen his love for her, but today she saw something she'd craved most of her adult life—his *respect*.

"I suppose you'll need the title, too," he said. "I'll dig it out of the safe and sign it over to you the next time you're at the house."

Sandra nodded, although she'd already decided her father could keep the title. She planned to return the prized car to him, eventually.

She kissed the keys in her palm. "You're *my* girl-friend now."

Everyone at the table broke out in a small round of laughter and applause, and Sandra was relieved to see her father join in.

Now that the bet was settled there was one thing left to do, Sandra thought, channeling the pride and dignity her client Octavia Hall had displayed after her dress fitting.

Sandra retrieved another bottle of wine. She waited for everyone to refill their glasses, before raising hers and proposing a toast.

"To Isaiah." She swallowed hard and hoped her voice wouldn't betray her and reveal her anguish. "A good person, a good son and a good friend. Best of luck in London."

Chapter 16

Hours later, Sandra's toast rang in Isaiah's head as he parked his truck in his parents' garage.

"...a good friend."

He had no right to feel slighted. After all, they'd been proclaiming they were simply good friends all over town. Nothing more.

"...a good friend."

It hurt, because with those words, Isaiah knew she'd let him go. Now what they'd tried so hard to convince everyone else of was true.

He and Sandra Woolcott were indeed just friends.

Isaiah exhaled, jumped out of his truck and shut the door behind him. After spending nearly every night since Halloween at Sandra's place, he'd decided to stay the last night with his folks. He'd told himself, and Sandra, it was to have some extra time with them before he left. In reality, Isaiah knew sleeping alone tonight would make it easier tomorrow to do the same thing for Sandra that she'd done for him.

Let go.

Isaiah walked through the back door to find his parents in the kitchen. His father was at the counter, pouring coffee into two mugs.

"Coffee, son?" he asked.

Isaiah nodded and sat at the table across from his mother. Not that he wanted coffee at this hour. He actually enjoyed their company and would miss them while he was in London.

"Decaf okay?"

"That would be great, Dad."

Ben placed a mug in front of his wife and another in front of Isaiah before retrieving one for himself.

Isaiah watched his mother wrap both hands around her mug and stare at the contents. Finally, she looked up.

"So you're really leaving in the morning?"

"I am." It would be difficult leaving his folks. However, it would be especially hard walking away from Sandra, *again*.

"I thought—" his mother began, but his father interrupted.

"Don't, Cecily," Ben said. "We've interfered in his life enough. Our son has his own dreams. We can't keep forcing ours on him."

Undeterred, Cecily focused her gaze on Isaiah. "But I thought all the time you spent both at Martine's and with Sandra might have changed your mind," she said. "I was thinking we could take the company off the market, and it would stay in the family, after all. After seeing you and Sandra together at Darren Howerton's victory party, I'd expected you two to announce your engagement tonight. So had Nancy."

Isaiah's short stint at their family business had made him think of Martine's potential. And after the furniture designs he and Sandra had created, Isaiah had indeed entertained the idea of totally revamping the company to produce simple pieces that were both useful and beautiful.

But he couldn't tell his mother. It would only give her hope, when there was none.

"No," Isaiah said.

One word that left no room for debate.

Tonight, Sandra had made it clear, despite the wonderful month they'd shared, that she was ready to move on. He had to do the same.

Sandra was his past. His future was in London.

His father put down his coffee mug and reached for his wife's hand. He looked at Isaiah, his dark brown eyes sad. "I have to admit, I'd also hoped for some kind of announcement from you and Sandra. I saw the way she looks at you, and how your look at her," he said. "No doubt you two would have been together for years now if I hadn't interfered. Perhaps by now you'd have even provided your mother and me with a couple of grandkids."

Isaiah swallowed a lump of emotion rising to his throat. "Don't, Dad," he said. "It was a long time ago. Sandra and I have moved on. You should, too."

Ben nodded. "So what time do you need a lift to the airport in the morning?"

"Sandra is dropping me off." Isaiah forced a smile. "She still owes me a ride in old man Woolcott's Chevelle."

* * *

Despite the cold early-morning temperatures, Sandra found Isaiah and his parents standing on the wraparound porch of their home when she roared up the driveway.

She moved to shut off the Chevelle's powerful engine, but stopped when she saw Cecily pull her son into one last hug, and Isaiah stride toward the car.

He wore jeans, his leather jacket and a New England Patriots cap on his head. Sandra soaked in every detail. Sleeping without him beside her last night had been a hard preview of the cold, empty nights to come.

She pressed her lips together hard. Once again, she summoned the pride and dignity Octavia Hall had eventually displayed in finally letting her estranged husband go.

Yet as Sandra watched Isaiah toss a leather duffel into the backseat of her newly won car, and slide into the passenger seat, all she wanted to do was beg him to stay.

"Is that it?" She looked away from him, so her face wouldn't reveal the turmoil of emotions swirling inside her.

"I travel light."

His words resonated as she backed out of the Jacobses' driveway and headed in the direction of Boston's Logan International Airport.

Isaiah was finally off to follow a dream he'd had for over a decade, and she couldn't hold him back. Asking him to stay in Wintersage for her, for them, wasn't fair to him.

If she loved him, the best thing she could do for him was what she'd been trying to do since yesterday—just let go.

"I meant what I said in my toast yesterday," she said. "You've been a great friend to me, Isaiah, and I really do wish you all the best. I hope art school is everything you wanted and more."

He covered the hand she didn't have on the steering wheel with his larger one, and gently squeezed it. "I hope so, too."

"Well, what do you think of my new wheels?" Sandra struggled to keep her tone upbeat.

Isaiah leaned forward in the pristine leather passenger's seat and glanced around the car's interior. "Sweet," he said. "So how long before you give her back to your father?"

Sandra blinked, then laughed. "How did you know I planned to return the car to him?"

"Because I know how much you love that old goat," he said. "I also always understood that this bet was never about winning a car for you."

No. It hadn't been, Sandra thought. Isaiah had realized it from the very beginning.

"My plan is to return it to him for his birthday in February. I figure three months is enough time for me to enjoy bragging rights."

Then she remembered one thing that had gotten lost in the hubbub around yesterday's dinner. "Thank you for helping me, Isaiah. I couldn't have pulled it off without you."

She felt the warmth of his smile. "I just enjoyed spending time together," he said.

She had, too, Sandra thought. More than she'd even intended.

A sign at the town's border announcing they were leaving Wintersage caught her attention, and Sandra diverted her gaze from it, hoping to find comfort in the monotony of the road. Instead, a sense of déjà vu came over her.

"Do you remember..." Isaiah began.

Sandra nodded before he could finish. "You taking me for a ride on this road the day you got your driver's license."

"I thought about it when I first got back, and then I saw you later that day at The Quarterdeck," he said.

"I thought about you earlier that day, too," she confessed. "A memory of the first time we met, in art class, just hit me out of the blue."

"So what do you think it means?" Isaiah asked.

Stay. Sandra bit down on her tongue to keep the word from escaping.

"Just overactive imaginations, I guess." She shrugged it off with a casualness she didn't come close to feeling.

An awkward silence fell over them, belying the easy camaraderie they'd shared during their month-long affair. It continued to haunt them as the airport came into view.

"I can park and come inside," Sandra offered, although she knew it would be torture watching him walk through Security to a plane and his new life.

Isaiah shook his head. "I think it'd be best if you just drop me off at the curb for Departures."

Willing the tears pressing against the back of her eyes not to appear, Sandra did as he suggested.

"Here you go." She put the car in Park at the curb, but kept the engine running. She reached deep to be the friend to him that he'd been to her, and send him off with a smile.

"Goodbye, Isaiah."

"Goodbye, Sandra." He leaned across the gearshift, held her face between his palms and brushed an achingly sweet kiss across her lips. "We've always been the right couple. You've always been the right woman. It's just never been the right time for us."

Sandra watched as he retrieved his bag from the backseat, walked through the airport's sliding glass doors and out of her life.

Chapter 17

Isaiah had dreamed of this moment.

From his years at Annapolis through his stint in the navy, he'd fantasized about attending one of the world's top art schools and having the freedom to paint all day, every day.

"Have a nice flight, sir." The airline agent checked him in and returned Isaiah's ticket.

Now the long-held dream was within his reach. All he had to do was go through the airport's security checkpoint and grab it.

Just go, man.

He followed the silent order, but the closer he got to the line, the more his sure stride faltered. He felt he was moving in slow motion as images of Sandra dogged every step.

The day they'd first met, in art class at Wintersage Academy.

Sitting beside her on a cliff overlooking the ocean as teenagers.

Running headfirst into a goalpost the first time he'd seen her in a cheerleader uniform.

Making love to her against her entryway wall the last time he'd seen her in a cheerleader uniform.

Isaiah's steps grew even slower as the images continued to bombard him at lightning speed. Only they weren't just images. They were memories. New ones they'd created together over the past month.

Sandra's cayenne-infused French toast.

Sandra's bubbly enthusiasm for her work.

Combining their love of fashion and art to work up sketches of what Martine's Fine Furnishings could have been.

All were sweet, wonderful memories that had become Isaiah's daily routine. Just like cooking dinner with her every evening and sharing a bed with her every night.

Isaiah stopped as realization dawned. Just as he'd made new memories the past month, he'd also found a new dream.

He let out a long, labored sigh and tossed his plane ticket in the nearby paper-recycling bin. He sucked in a gulp of fresh air filled with hope for the future, and walked briskly to the rental car counter.

He prayed it wasn't too late.

Later that evening, Sandra drove the Chevelle, packed with Janelle, Vicki and as many shopping bags as they could fit into it, back to the Victorian.

After dropping Isaiah off at the airport, all she'd wanted to do was go to her office at Swoon and work until she was too tired to think. Too exhausted to hurt.

However, Janelle and Vicki had refused to take no for an answer and practically dragged her out of the office, insisting she accompany them on a Black Friday shopping trip. She was grateful they had. Their spree had been fun, and it did take her mind off Isaiah. Just for a few hours.

"Will your quit staring at me and keep your eyes on the road?" Vicki yelled from the passenger's seat.

"I can't help it," Sandra insisted, taking in her friend's newly cropped hair. "You look…"

"Hot!" Janelle chimed in from the backseat. "It's about time you added a touch of makeup and let go of that schoolmarm bun."

"It wasn't a bun. It was a chignon, which was both—"

"Elegant and functional," Sandra and Janelle said simultaneously, using Vicki's description of the practical hairstyle.

"Seriously, Vicki, you look adorable," Sandra said.

Janelle leaned in from the back and stuck her head between the bucket seats. "Sandra's right. Your new look, combined with these hot new clothes you picked up, will net you more Mr. Rights than you can handle."

"I only need one." Vicki's voice took on a dreamy tone. "Hopefully, today's haircut, new makeup and clothes will lure him out of hiding."

Shopping bags rustled on the seat as Janelle sat back. "Sandra had me thinking she'd be the next one of us to marry, but with Isaiah gone, my money's on you to be the next one walking down the aisle."

Sandra's chest tightened at the mention of his name. It would be a long time before it stopped hurting each time she thought of him.

"I didn't believe it, but you and Isaiah were telling the truth about just being good friends, after all," Vicki said.

"Friends," Sandra said softly, trying to block out images of Isaiah, and his last sweet kiss.

"Who's that?" Vicki asked, as the Victorian came into view.

It was dark out, but the porch light of the house was on.

"I don't see anyone," Janelle said.

"Me, either." Sandra looked down the street and along the sidewalk.

"There's a man on our porch," Vicki said.

"In this weather?" Janelle sounded skeptical. "It's thirty degrees outside."

Sandra parked the Chevelle in front of the house.

"Over there," Vicki insisted.

A tall, dark figure emerged from the shadows, and Sandra's breath caught. She'd know that body anywhere. But it couldn't be him, she thought. Isaiah had no doubt landed in London by now. She was just imagining things, as she had that night at The Quarterdeck.

Only she *hadn't* imagined him at the restaurant.

"It's Isaiah," Vicki said as he came into view, confirming it.

"I thought you said he left," Janelle commented.

Sandra got out of the car as he approached, resisting the urge to meet him halfway and fling her arms around him.

"What are you doing here?" she asked.

By now her friends had tumbled out the car and were standing behind her.

"Evening, Janelle, Vicki." Isaiah greeted them and

then turned his attention back to her. "I have a business proposition I'd like to discuss with you."

"Business?" Sandra asked, disappointed. Her gaze traveled to the sketchbook under his arm.

When she'd realized it really was Isaiah standing on the porch, she'd mistakenly assumed he'd returned for her.

Just her.

Sandra nodded once and inclined her head toward the Victorian. "Let's go upstairs, and you can tell me all about it."

Janelle and Vicki, who had both planned to go directly home after they retrieved their cars, followed them inside. Janelle was on the staircase leading to Swoon when Vicki grabbed her by the arm.

"Hey, I wanted to hear what—" Janelle began.

"We'll be downstairs in Petals if you need us." Vicki steered her inside the flower shop.

Upstairs, Sandra switched on the track lights and took off her coat. "Can I make you a cup of coffee or something?" she asked. "It was much too cold for you to wait outside."

"I'm good. I was too anxious to speak with you to sit in a car or wait at my parents' place."

Sandra inclined her head toward the armchairs she used when consulting with clients. "So what's this all about?"

Isaiah declined her offer of a seat. "I have two propositions for you to consider," he said. "But there's no pressure for you to make decisions on them right away, just some things I'd like you to think over."

"Okay." Now Sandra was curious. Business propositions? What kind of business could he want to discuss with her? Surely he didn't need an evening gown.

Isaiah held out the sketch pad. "Open it."

Sandra took it and began flipping through the pages. "It's the furniture designs we were playing around with the other night."

She glanced up to see an eager smile spread across his lips. "Turn to the last page."

Sandra did as he asked, then gasped. "Oh, my God." She looked from the sketchbook page to Isaiah and back again.

"So what do you think?" he asked.

Sandra stared at the logo painted in watercolor.

"Swoon Couture Home by Martine's Fine Furnishings," she read aloud.

"As I've said before, you have a good eye, great taste and we made a fantastic team."

"B-but how? I mean…" Sandra stammered, trying to absorb it all.

"As of this afternoon, I'm the company's new president and cocreative director," he said.

"Cocreative director?"

"I'd like you on board to work by my side as the other creative director." He glanced around Swoon's headquarters. "In addition to your duties here, of course."

"But your art?" Sandra asked.

"I'll still be creating art, just using a new medium," Isaiah said.

Much the way she felt about the man in front of her, Sandra fell in love with the idea.

She studied the logo again, and then met Isaiah's hopeful gaze.

"Do we have a deal?" he asked.

Sandra extended her hand. "Deal."

He exhaled as he took it. "Now for the other proposition," he said.

Sandra's eyes rounded, and she shook her head. "But I'm going to be stretched thin enough designing dresses and now a furniture collection. I simply don't have time to take on designing anything else."

"Just hear me out," Isaiah said. "If you still say you can't do it, I'll understand."

She nodded, although she already knew there weren't enough hours in the day to take on another design task.

"There's one last thing I'd like you to design—a life for us as man and wife." Isaiah reached in his pocket and pulled out an emerald ring surrounded by diamonds, which Sandra had seen on Cecily's hand. "This ring once belonged to my great-grandmother, then my grandmother and mother. Now I want you to wear it."

Sandra heard a rustling sound at the closed door.

"Say yes!" Janelle squealed from the other side.

Sandra and Isaiah erupted into laughter.

"Yes," Sandra said, when their laughter finally subsided.

Isaiah slid the ring on her finger and then pulled her into his arms. "You've always been the right girl. Our time is now," he said. "I love you, Sandra."

Her heart melted under the intensity of his dark gaze. "I love you, too."

Moments later, there was more rustling at the door. "Enough already with the kissing. You have a lifetime of that ahead of you," Vicki said. "Let us in!"

Isaiah leaned in for one more kiss before finally releasing her. Sandra yanked open the door. Janelle and

Vicki, who apparently had their ears pressed against it, tumbled inside.

Once they righted themselves, Janelle immediately reached for her hand. "What a beautiful ring," she exclaimed.

"It belonged to Isaiah's great-grandmother," Sandra said proudly.

"We heard." Vicki smiled, and then pulled her into a hug. "Congratulations. I always knew he was your Prince Charming," she whispered against her ear.

Janelle hugged her in turn and then Isaiah. "Congratulations to you both," she said. "When can I start planning the wedding?"

Isaiah slipped an arm around Sandra and pulled her close. "Thanks, but there's no time for a wedding. I'm making Sandra my wife tonight."

She smiled up at him in agreement.

"B-but there *has* to be a wedding," Vicki stammered.

"We don't want to wait," Sandra said. "We've already waited ten years."

Janelle raised a brow. "You're going to have to wait, because the earliest you two can get a marriage license is Monday, and then after that there's a three-day waiting period in Massachusetts."

"And don't you two even think of hopping on a plane to Las Vegas," Vicki warned.

Sandra sighed.

"Okay, we'll get married on Thursday," Isaiah said. "But we're not waiting a second longer."

"And it has to be on the beach." Sandra looked up at him.

"The beach?" Janelle asked incredulously.

Vicki's jaw dropped. "In late November. In *Massachusetts*?"

"Right here on our beach in Wintersage," Isaiah confirmed.

"In November," Sandra seconded.

"Well, I guess we'd better get busy planning a wedding," Vicki said.

"Hold on a sec." Sandra suddenly remembered she had a dress to prepare for the governor-elect's wife. She quickly explained the situation to her friends. "So I don't have time to plan a wedding."

"Then Vegas it is," Isaiah declared.

"Oh, no, you don't," Vicki said. "Janelle and I will handle the wedding."

"But my dress?" Sandra had designed plenty of wedding gowns, but never once thought of what she'd want her own to look like.

"We'll take care of your dress," Vicki insisted. "We'll take care of everything."

Sandra looked from her to Janelle. "Do you really think you can pull it together by Thursday?"

Janelle placed her fist on her hip. "Alluring Affairs can pull off *anything*."

Chapter 18

Sandra looked up at the cliffs and wiggled her toes inside sequined Ugg boots as delicate flakes of falling snow clung to her eyelashes.

Given the option of moving the wedding indoors, both she and Isaiah had declined. They'd wanted to add this momentous occasion to the already special memories they'd created on this beach.

Holding on to her father's arm, Sandra took in the sight of Isaiah as she walked past her friends and their families to the arbor where he and a minister awaited.

As a teenager she'd believed she'd loved him with all her heart. Now she knew that was indeed just puppy love and nothing compared to the way she loved him now.

A gust of wind stirred up the light snow, but happiness was a buffer from the cold.

Also, Janelle and Vicki had outfitted her in the perfect wedding attire. Sandra was snuggled inside a short, faux-fur jacket she wore over a hand-crocheted column gown in a sumptuous yarn that felt both soft and luxurious against her skin.

She didn't even want to think of taking the beautiful gown off—until tonight…

"Be good to my baby, Jacobs." Stuart's gruff voice belied the smile on his face as he kissed Sandra's cheek and placed her hand in Isaiah's.

"Will do, sir," he assured him.

Isaiah turned to Sandra. She looked from the peach rose pinned on his cashmere overcoat, a perfect match to the ones she carried in her bouquet, to his smiling face.

Marry me, he silently mouthed.

Sandra nodded and they both faced the minister, who within several glorious minutes transformed high school sweethearts into husband and wife.

"You may now kiss your bride."

"Good!" Mason shouted from her brother's arms.

The small crowd erupted into laughter and applause as Isaiah captured her lips in a kiss and sealed the deal.

While the wedding ceremony had been small, most of Wintersage awaited them at the reception held at the town's recreation center, where Sandra had fallen into Isaiah's arms after being apart ten years. Janelle and Vicki had outdone themselves, Sandra thought, looking around. Orange linen cloths covered the tables, which were adorned with spectacular centerpieces fashioned from silk leaves in autumn colors reminiscent of Wintersage at peak season.

In lieu of a traditional wedding cake, her friends had

had Carrie from the bakery fashion one made entirely of peach-frosted cupcakes.

Sandra stood beside Isaiah in the receiving line as well-wishers congratulated them.

"I wish you all the best, dear." Octavia Hall embraced Sandra.

She thanked her and smiled when she saw a contrite-looking Mr. Hall standing next her.

Tony Green, who'd gone to school with them at Wintersage Academy, was the next to offer his congratulations, a handshake for Isaiah and a hug for Sandra.

"Looking forward to working with you," she said.

"Me, too," Tony declared. "I'm still reeling from the huge promotion you two gave me."

Isaiah placed a hand on his shoulder. "Well deserved," he said. "And my mother agrees we need fresh blood in the front offices at Martine's, someone who also knows the company."

As the line dwindled, Sandra scanned the room for her friends. She soon located Janelle in a corner, cozied up to her husband.

Finally, Sandra spotted Vicki, who she'd overlooked several times because she'd been searching for her old schoolmarm bun. Though it had been nearly a week, everyone was still adjusting to Vicki's chic makeover.

Then Sandra caught sight of someone else's eyes glued to her friend.

She nudged Isaiah with her elbow and inclined her head. "Do you see what I see?" she asked her new husband.

"I noticed it earlier," he said. "You can't miss it. Your brother's practically drooling."

"Well, well, well." Sandra grinned.

"Don't get ahead of yourself, sweetheart," Isaiah warned.

Too late, she thought, looking from her best friend to her brother.

Already, Sandra hoped for another wedding in Wintersage.

* * * * *

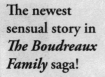